The Gospel
According to John Bill Bob Mark
A SMOKY MOUNTAIN VERSION
BASED ON AND ADAPTED FROM THE GOSPEL OF MARK

BY
BRUCE W. SPANGLER

© Copyright 2003 Bruce W. Spangler. All rights reserved.

No part of this publication may be reproduced, stored in a retrieval system, or transmitted, in any form or by any means, electronic, mechanical, photocopying, recording, or otherwise, without the written prior permission of the author.

Printed in Victoria, Canada

```
National Library of Canada Cataloguing in Publication Data

Spangler, Bruce W., 1956-
      The gospel according to John, Bill, Bob, Mark : a
Smoky Mountain version based upon and adapted from the
Gospel of Mark / Bruce W. Spangler.
ISBN 1-55395-883-7
      1. Christian fiction.  I. Title.
PS3619.P35G67 2003        813'.6         C2003-901142-9
```

TRAFFORD

This book was published *on-demand* in cooperation with Trafford Publishing.
On-demand publishing is a unique process and service of making a book available for retail sale to the public taking advantage of on-demand manufacturing and Internet marketing. **On-demand publishing** includes promotions, retail sales, manufacturing, order fulfilment, accounting and collecting royalties on behalf of the author.

Suite 6E, 2333 Government St., Victoria, B.C. V8T 4P4, CANADA
Phone   250-383-6864   Toll-free   1-888-232-4444 (Canada & US)
Fax   250-383-6804   E-mail   sales@trafford.com
Web site   www.trafford.com   TRAFFORD PUBLISHING IS A DIVISION OF TRAFFORD
HOLDINGS LTD.
Trafford Catalogue #03-0246   www.trafford.com/robots/03-0246.html

10   9   8   7   6   5   4   3   2   1

To my hillbilly kin both known and unknown

The Gospel According to John Bill Bob Mark
A SMOKY MOUNTAIN VERSION
BASED ON AND ADAPTED FROM
THE GOSPEL OF MARK

TABLE OF CONTENTS

ACKNOWLEDGEMENTS..........1

WORDS BEFORE HAND..........4

HIT'S DRESSIN' UP TIME--
THE COMMENCEMENT OF THE JESUS' PRACHIN'

(1:1)
A "Star" from the Beginnin'..........25
(1:2-13)
John Bob, the Baptizer..........26
(1:14-22)
Hit's Dressin' Up Time!..........30
(1:23-27)
A Change of Heart..........34
(1:28-39)
In Need of More Than Just a Poultice..........36
(1:40-45)
God Loves Even Dram Drinkers..........39

TRASHY TALK

(2:1-13)
Junior Drives a Pick-Up..41
(2:14-22)
Gene--A New Hillbilly..45
(2:23-28)
Silver Queen and the Blue Laws....................................49
(3:1-5)
"That Sucker is as Goot as New!"................................51
(3:6-7)
The Loyal Minority...52
(3:8-13)
Tellin' the Goot News of Freedom................................53
(3:13-20)
Commissionin' of the Goot News Hillbillies................55
(3:21-35)
Trash Talk..56

TELLIN' THE STORIES OF THE GOOT NEWS

(4:1-9)
The Poke With Dropsy..61
(4:9-23)
What's the Difference Between a Loaf of Bread
　　　and a Rhode Island Red?..62
(4:24-29)
You Get What You Put Into It!....................................64
(4:30-36)
Freedom is Like an Apple Seed....................................65

MIRACLES AROUND DOUGLAS LAKE

(4:37-41)
Shorty Forgets His AM Radio..67
(5:1-20)
A White Capped Bubba...68
(5:21-43)
A Family Crest...72

MORE PRACHIN' BY JESUS

(6:1-6)
Sunday Prachin'...79
(6:7-14)
The Tradition of the Walkin' Stick............................80
(6:15-31)
Myles Horton or Nostradamus..81
(6:32-44)
Service with a Smile
      and Faster Than Mickey D's......................85
(6:45-56)
Light-Struck Possums..87
(7:1-23)
Ode to the Old Brown Shack Out Back......................89
(7:24-30)
A Yankee Visits Jesus..92
(7:31-37)
The Cost of Freedom..94
(8:1-13)
Dinner on the Ground..96
(8:14-26)
A Discourse on
      Bread, Chickens, and Everythang Else.........99

v

PREPARIN' GOD'S HILLBILLIES

(8:27-38)
Billy Graham, Oral Roberts, Benny Hinn, Home
        Grown 'Maters and Rhode Island Reds.......101

(9:1-13)
Jesus, Johns, Parks, and Jordan--What a Team!....104

(9:14-30)
A Young Boy at Ripley's...106

(9:31-50)
"Watch Out for the Hornets' Nest".........................109

(10:1-16)
"Why are You Worried About Burnt Biscuits?"....113

(10:17-27)
"You Can't Holt a Baby with Your Arms Full"....115

(10:28-31)
"I Ain't Got No Dime Now".......................................118

(10:32-45)
Those Pesky Hornets..118

(10:46-52)
Ernest and Curious George...121

FINAL DAYS IN KNOXVUL

(11:1-25)
Rambilin' Towards Knoxvul.......................................123

(11:26-33)
Don't Ever Say Somethin' Bad
                      About My Family...........126

(12:1-12)
Muskedine Wine and Other Whines........................127

(12:13-37)
Uncle Sam and Other Hounds That Chase...............128

(12:38-44)
"Give Until You Starve"
                and Other Misquotes of God..................134

(13:1-37)
Sticks and Stones..135

LYNCHED IN JAIL AND CRUCIFIED IN THE PAPERS

(14:1-9)
The Rose of Sharin'...138
(14:10-17)
The Plot and Gravy Thickens.................................139
(14:18-26)
"Rocky Top"..140
(14:27-42)
Hit's Hard to Pray with a Full Belly.........................142
(14:43-52)
Hit's Time to Test the Gravy..................................144
(14:52-72)
Guilty as Sin and Just as Ugly.................................145
(15:1-47)
Crucified in the Papers...147

"HE AIN'T HERE"

(16:1-8)
He Ain't Here
        and Thangs are Goin' to Be Different......150
(16:9-19)
Postscript..151

WORDS AFTER HAND..154

ACKNOWLEDGMENTS

There have been numerous people along the way that have influenced the writing of ***The Gospel According to John Bill Bob Mark, A Smoky Mountain Version.*** Far too numerous to mention, however, are those who have influenced and challenged me to embrace my heritage. To those unnamed ones, I bow in grateful appreciation and sincere indebtedness.

I extend words of appreciation to Dr. James Philpott who was an early reader and encourager to complete this task. He has come to serve both as a mentor and advisor, but always insists on being my friend.

Dr. James Logan at Wesley Theological Seminary continues to "school" me on the "structure" of God's story. His pastoral style of teaching will forever feed and challenge me.

Dr. James Clemons, also at Wesley Theological Seminary, has served as an ardent advisor of both detail and style of this work. He also has reminded me of an enthusiasm and passion for one's own lineage and pedigree. I am indebted to him for his time and patience.

The following folks served as readers in the early stages of this project.

To Millie Sieber and Jim Murphy, I offer my apologies for such a "rough" technical presentation.

Your willingness to navigate through numerous typos and grammatical errors deserves more recognition that I offer in this small space.

Rev. Brenda Carroll, Rev. Larry Dial, and Rev. Sullins Lamb are all clergy peers with tons of pastoral love and encouragement who were generous, gracious, and frank in their remarks.

Mary Frances Marlin is both a grandmother I never had and a person of faith that I aspire to mirror.

Sharon Leathermann did a big favor of reviewing and commenting during a difficult time in her life.

Dolores Wood not only served as reader, she also helped in creating the evaluation form. She has taught me plenty about "community."

Rita Arni, the only "non-resident" hillbilly, graciously offered kind, loving and helpful words in her typical courteous and "Midwestern-plains" style.

I also thank Evelyn Wood for taking the time to proofread an earlier version. However, any errors found within are mine because I either neglected or overlooked her helpful advice.

I dedicated this project to five people.

Phyllis, my companion, continues to encourage, support and tolerant my ramblings. She has already served her penitence for the life to come.

I also dedicate it to John and Evelyn Spangler, my loving parents. My family continues to remind me of an unconditional love. They also serve as a wellspring of refreshing joy and laughter.

Staley McPeak, a true hillbilly with the mind of Einstein, receives this dedication for not only his support of my personal ministry as a Methodist cleric, but also his humor, wit, and "down right smartness." He has taught me a little about the myth of "unsweet" which I continue to perpetuate. His friendship, however, has taught me much about life and acceptance.

Finally, I include Dr. Denise Hopkins, also of Wesley Theological Seminary, in this list of dedications. In an indirect way, her enlivening spirit of affirmation of a previous writing gave me the "creative edge" along the months of writing.

The Gospel According to John Bill Bob Mark
A SMOKY MOUNTAIN VERSION
BASED ON AND ADAPTED FROM THE GOSPEL OF MARK

WORDS BEFORE HAND

O for a thousand tongues to sing my great Redeemer's praise, the glories of my God and King, the triumphs of his grace![1]

Charles Wesley

It all commences with the good news of one of God's "stars," about God's hillbilly, Jesus the Christ, and hit all starts in God's country, the Great Smoky Mountains of southern Appalachia. Some have suggested these parts surely must belong to God because "no one but God would have it!" That's only partially true.

The Gospel According to John Bill Bob Mark,
A Smoky Mountain Version (SMV)

When the Church of God gets to talking it doesn't talk in unknown tongues. It talks in the tongues of people. It talks in their native dialect. It knows how to talk "hippie." It knows how to talk "lay[person]." It knows how to talk "ministerial." It knows how to talk bum language. It knows how to talk presidential language. It knows how to talk all kinds of language. The spirit of God becomes articulate and speaks the language of people. It doesn't get up in the church with a holy whine and talk about "thee" and "thou" and "what" and "what-not." When the Church becomes articulate, it becomes articulate in the language in which

---

[1] Charles Wesley, "O For a Thousand Tongues to Sing," found in *The United Methodist Hymnal* (Nashville, Tennessee: The United Methodist Publishing House, 1989), 57.

people are born - not some foreign, ministerial kind of language.[2]
The Substance of Faith and other Cotton Patch Sermons,
Clarence Jordan

With a thousand tongues with which to offer praise unto his God, Charles Wesley would have them all versify in and with a single voice. For Clarence Jordan, however, a thousand tongues doesn't begin to note God's linguistic talents--God is not "tongue-challenged." God can prattle with the best and worst of us all.

From "hippie" and the "bum" to "ministerial," from ordinary church folk to the clattering of ecclesiastical and presidential doublespeak, God gets the word out and across. From Galilee of first century Palestine to twenty-first century Knoxville, Tennessee, USA, from the desert southwest sands of New Mexico to the frigid icy land of Greenland, and from the vastness of the continent of Africa to the hollers of the Smoky Mountains, God gets the "Word" out about grace, hope and an empowering freedom.

This "Smoky Mountain Version" (SMV) of the Gospel of Mark is about getting the "Word" out--hillbilly style.

It begins with John Bob the Baptizer appearing on Rich Mountain in Townsend, Tennessee of the Great Smoky Mountains. In these

---

[2] Clarence Jordan, *The Substance of Faith and other Cotton Patch Sermons by Clarence Jordan,* ed. Dallas Lee (New York: Association Press, 1972), 23.

mountains, located in the southern region of Appalachia with popular culture "knowing" these parts as "hillbilly country," John Bob begins with a baptism of preparation because God is *"about to do somethin' special in these parts."* John Bob is only preparing the way, however.

Jesus arrives from Newport, Tennessee and comes to be baptized by John Bob.

The good news of God is now off and running--running as fast as "swelled and muddy river water."

This Jesus, however, is distinctively Wesleyan and Appalachian in this version. He calls people to acknowledge and accept the offer of God's justifying freedom as an experienced love and to participate in the challenge of God's sanctifying freedom that transforms both the individual and the world. God's freedom begins by "freeing" the person to "be," simply. Furthermore, God transforms the individual into one of God's loving "hillbillies." God redeems and reconstitutes the community for the purpose of nurture, care and challenge--with a hillbilly flavor.

Using the style of "Jack Tales," a storytelling technique of Appalachia, the SMV appropriates a Wesleyan demonstration of God's present, saving and transforming grace in the Jesus of Mark's gospel.

But why the SMV?

Hopefully, it is a story of "thanks" unto a

God that is not "tongue-limited" nor "hillbilly-challenged."

One underlying theory or presupposition of this work is that the Gospel of Mark is a literary endeavor by first-century Palestine Christianity to present, frame and contextualize an expression of faith in and to a culture that is predominantly oral in its make-up. Quite different from the earlier Pauline, pseudo-Pauline, and Johnannine literature of direct discourse of "letters and homilies," Mark's narrative story-telling form *"helps the reader hear the voices, take part in the action, get involved in the plot, identify with characters....[enabling] the reader to be caught up into the narrative as a participant."* [3] The Gospel of Mark begins with a distinct and provocative pronouncement, *"[t]he beginning of the good news of Jesus Christ, the Son of God."* It commences with not only a proclamation of religious intent, it echoes with a voice of political and social savvy.

Shortly before the birth of Jesus, the term of "good news" was found in Roman imperial inscriptions with the explicit purpose of reminding, informing, and promoting the constituency of citizens and inhabitants of the *"peace brought by the rule of the emperor"* and the *"inaugurating of a new age."* [4] Confronted with conflicting loyalties between the

---

[3] Dennis C. Dulling and Norman Perrin, *The New Testament: Proclamation and Parenesis, Myth and History*. (Fort Worth, Texas: Harcourt Brace College Publishers, 1994), 325.
[4] Ibid., 295.

demands of Caesar's realm and God's domain, how and why did this early Christian community come to terms with its choice of God over Caesar, Jerusalem over Rome?

Mark reminds his community of the continuing story--the story of God and God's actions in history.

With the constant dilemma of competing loyalties, the readers/listeners of Mark would have understood the political and social significance of Jesus casting the spirit of "Legion" into the swine and running the herd over the cliff.[5] Though tacitly understanding the existing political quandary of God's "good news" over Caesar's "good news," Mark's gospel is neither a dissertation to describe this "good news" of God or a treatise. Mark tells a story.

The form and use of story-telling not only articulates and conveys a wide-spread existential angst or sigh that is too abstract and too hidden to express, it forms and crystallizes the accepted axiom that God abhors injustices of the world, and God can and will do something about it. Tex Sample offers a rather blunt, but yet effective example, of this sentiment when he quotes a "hard-living" and "oral-based" Christian believer as saying that, *"Jesus is coming and he is coming to kick ass."* [6]

---

[5] See Mark 5:1ff.

[6] Tex Sample, *Ministry in an Oral Culture: Living with Will Rogers, Uncle*

If you were to ask the sentiments of any Appalachian "old-timer" removed from the mountains as the United States government established a national park, you would probably get a similar response. The response, however, may begin with a preface, *"We never axed to be nephews and nieces of no Uncle Sam!"*

In Appalachia one can now hear a parallel story of a "devil" cloaked, not in Roman attire, however, but fully signified in the red, white, and blue pinstripes of an "Uncle Sam." With "Uncle Sam" the "good news" is always "goot" [7] for himself not the hillbilly.

The Smoky Mountain National Park brought protection to virgin timbers and visitors to the mountains. The Tennessee Valley Authority (TVA) introduced flood control, indoor plumbing and electricity to the southern region of Appalachia. There remains, however, feelings of cynicism, mistrust, and distrust of anything or anyone associated with "Uncle Sam."

For the Christians of the Gospel of Mark, "Legion" and Rome are the nemeses.

For some Christians in Appalachia, there are "Uncle Sam" and Washington, D.C..

What comes of one's world-view when property and home are just commodities to be

---

Remus, and Minnie Pearl. (Louisville, Kentucky: W/JKP, 1994), 25.
[7] Good.

manipulated in the hands of the "Caesar" of the day? What impact does this experience have upon one's faith? How does that impact get articulated and expressed in an oral culture of people who have faith in an active God who frees?

The Gospel of Mark is a written document of a predominantly oral culture that contextualized the experience of a God who loves, redeems and who frees by the power of transformation through a grace that has real practical effects in the lives of real people.

This is what Mark is about.

This is what the SMV is all about, as well.

What, however, are the "grammatical rules" of God's story?

What is the pattern, the order of the revelation of the nature and activity of this God that sends Jesus? The gospel of story is known in the life, death, and resurrection of Jesus. God's story of life over death in the scriptures "precedes" all other stories. It is important to note, therefore, the "grammar" of the biblical tradition.

Walter Brueggemann suggests that the "text" of God's story is "so *powerful and compelling, so passionate and uncompromising in its anguish and hope that it requires we submit our experience to it and thereby reenter our experience on new terms, namely the terms of the text.*" [8]

---

[8] Walter Brueggemann, *A Commentary on Jeremiah: Exile and Homecoming*. (Grand Rapids, Michigan: William B. Eerdmans Publishing Company, 1998), 18.

The faith tradition of the biblical record, therefore, requires that one "submit" experience to the text for interpretation, not vise versa. The SMV "submits" to the "authority" of God's story. It is the gospel story that is the "subject and verb." The SMV, at best can only be the "direct object." It can only be "constructive" and "instructive" as the result of the action of God's story telling. The SMV does not "direct" the story of God. The story of God "directs" the SMV.

It is not enough just to "know" the world of Jesus, nor simply our own world, *"[s]ince meaning occurs in the interaction between the text and those who receive it, and is not defined or delimited by the text alone, each new occasion with a text will create new meanings."* [9] This assumption is that the "truth" of scripture emerges from the intersection of reader and text. Therefore, "truth" is not a kernel that has to be extracted from the shell of superfluous sheathing, and whose only purpose is to "protect" and "guard" the integrity of its core. Such "shelling" presupposes that the casing is dispensable and of no value apart from its intrinsic value of insulation. "Truth" emerges out of relationships, *"[m]eaning thus occurs not in isolated words or signs, but in the relationships of those words within and between the worlds..."* [10]

---

[9] Frederick C. Tiffany and Sharon H. Ringe. *Biblical Interpretation: A Roadmap* (Nashville: Abingdon Press,1996), 27.
[10] Ibid., 27.

As the story of God intersects southern Appalachia, the SMV expresses that relation in light of a Wesleyan perspective. This Jesus of the SMV appeals to the power of God's grace, mercy, and love to empower people to "be." In a culture of repression, oppression, and submission, God's freeing grace comes to life in the form of people affirming and choosing their own personhood and history.

A Wesleyan Perspective of Salvation

John Wesley, Anglican priest and founder of an eighteenth century Church of England renewal movement (acrimoniously named "Methodist" by opponents, adversaries and other critics), describes his understanding of God's saving grace in a *via salutis*, i.e., an order of salvation, in his sermon, "The Scripture Way of Salvation." He declares that the purpose of God's saving grace is to restore the divine moral image of love within humanity through God's grace that is *"preventing, convicting, justifying,* and *sanctifying - and in this life time"*:

...What is salvation? The salvation which is here spoken of is not what is frequently understood by that word, the going to heaven, eternal happiness. It is not the soul's going to paradise, termed our Lord 'Abraham's bosom.' It is not a blessing which lies on the other side of death, or (as we usually speak) in the other world...It is not something at a distance; it is a present thing, a blessing which, through the free mercy of God, ye are now in possession of....So that the salvation which is here spoken of might be extended to the entire work of God, from the first dawning of grace in the soul till it is consummated in glory.[11]

In other words, God's salvation is a present reality. God's desire for God's creation is a "blessing" of "being" for the present. Noted Wesleyan scholar, Kenneth Collins points out that the principal and key motif in Wesley's theology lies not only in his weaving of various doctrines and principles into a single systematic, yet folksy system, but what *"lies behind them as their source and context - the grace of God."* [12] This grace, this *"undeserved favour of God,"* not only has the power to redeem, it restores, heals and transforms the moral image of humanity that has been tainted and corrupted by the lack of love.[13] Whereas Augustine understood the "Fall" of humanity in the Genesis story as an act of desire and disobedience, Wesley perceives it as *"lack of love."* [14]

In his sermon "Original Sin," Wesley defines the essence and being of sin as *"original and inbred."* Affecting our *"tempers"* and will to *"love the world,"* [15] sin results in humanity's bent towards the *"disease of*

---

[11] John Wesley, "The Scripture Way of Salvation" *John Wesley's Sermons: An Anthology*, ed. Albert C. Outler and Richard P. Heitzenrater, (Nashville: Abingdon Press, 1991), 372. All subsequent John Wesley sermon references are from this volume and are noted with the title of the sermon and page reference.

[12] Kenneth J. Collins, *The Scripture Way of Salvation: The Heart of John Wesley's Theology*. (Nashville: Abingdon Press, 1997), 19.

[13] Ibid.

[14] Melvin E. Dieter, et al. *Five Views on Sanctification*. (Grand Rapids, MI: Zondervan Publishing House, 1987), 22-3.

[15] "Original Sin," 332.

illusion of self-sufficiency." [16] This delusion of independence is both symptomatic and problematic of a moral character corrupted. Sin is the proposition or state of being that an individual need not, cannot, or will not be "beholden" to another being--either God or neighbor. The effect of sin is that it not only separates individual from God and individual from individual, but that separation debilitates the faculties to love or be loved, extend compassion, be empathic, and strive for peace with justice. Subsequently, sin has corrupted the *"moral image."* [17]

Though the *"natural and political images"* are corrupted as well, the "Fall" did not totally diminish humanity's *"spiritual nature and immorality of the soul"* nor lose *"dominion over the creatures."* [18] Humanity still has the God-given capacity to recognize the spiritual dimension of life and to organize life politically, socially and economically. It's inability and unwillingness to establish political life, social life and economic life for the sake of **all** is indicative of this corrupted moral character--the lack of love:

> Why must we be born again? What is the foundation of this doctrine? The foundation of it lies near as deep as the creation of the world; in the scriptural account whereof we read, "And God,

---

[16] Ibid., 326.

[17] Randy L. Maddox, *Responsible Grace: John Wesley's Practical Theology.* (Nashville: Kingswood Press, 1994), 93.

[18] Harald Lindstrom, *Wesley and Sanctification.* (Nappanee, IN: Francis Asbury Press, 1996), 44.

the three-one God, said, "Let us make man [sic.] in our image, after our likeness. So God created man in his own image, in the image of God created he him:" Not barely in his natural image, a picture of his own immortality; a spiritual being, endued with understanding, freedom of will, and various affections; --nor merely in his political image, the governor of this lower world, having "dominion over the fishes of the sea, and over all the earth";--but chiefly in his moral image; which, according to the Apostle, is "righteousness and true holiness." In this image of God was man made. "God is love:" Accordingly, man at his creation was full of love; which was the sole principle of all his tempers, thoughts, words, and actions. God is full of justice, mercy, and truth; so was man as he came from the hands of his Creator. God is spotless purity; and so man was in the beginning pure from every sinful blot; otherwise God could not have pronounced him, as well as all the other work of his hands, "verygood." [19]

From the beginning, the presence of God's *"preventing"* grace is always with us--a grace interwoven and endowed in the very fabric of life. Created in the natural image of God, humanity is *"endowed...with a measure of free will and some power of discernment"* that makes it *"possible for humanity to seek God."* [20]

The work of God's *"convicting"* grace awakens and stirs humanity to recognize its collective and inherited *"poverty of spirit,"* i.e., sin and guilt. Freedom from the shame of "who we are" is the work of God's "justifying" grace. It has both *"judicial and therapeutic"* natures.[21] It acknowledges

---

[19] "The New Birth," 336-7.
[20] Ibid., 45-6.
[21] Maddox, 143.

God's reconciliation recognized in what Christ has done for both humanity and the world. Christ's death is an atonement for us, not God. Forgiveness, pardon and new birth are the characteristics of this grace that frees the individual from the prior effects of the collective, inherited, and objective guilt. Simultaneously, however, it is the beginning of the curing and healing of the subjective, personal guilt, or shame.[22] The experience of God's grace is also therapeutic in its nature. It involves not only forgiveness and pardon, but also it promotes and brings healing.[23] This healing aspect is described as *"sanctifying"* grace.

Whereas justification is *"what God has done for us,"* sanctification is *"what God is doing in us."* It confronts not just the inherited guilt or shame, but the personal, existential reality of *who we are*--our character. Sanctifying grace is the act of God *"implanting"* within us the *"seeds"* of love, justice, and compassion, that frees the individual from the *"root of sin,"* i.e., pride, wrath, foolish desires or the claim that one is not "lovable." Through the experience of God's grace, however, life is redirected by love, not self-interest. With God implanting new tempers

---

[22] Whereas Wesley speaks of "guilt," I wonder if a more contemporary and accurate term should be "shame." For me, guilt implies the resulting emotion from wrong actions, i.e., guilt results from "what I do." Shame, on the other hand, speaks more of "who I am." I think that this definition gets more at the root of what Wesley is suggesting in "personal guilt."

[23] See Maddox, 145.

in the will. The will is remedied by the working of God's love. As a result of God's love, we are capable of *"responding to and welcoming God's further transforming work in [our life]...."* [24] Sanctification is about changing, reclaiming and restoring the human nature, in particular, humanity's moral image. It is progressive change from being loved to being one that loves. It is the "ethical" transformation of the heart and life of humanity and love is the essence of that transformation.[25]

The essence of sanctification is love in action, with love as the final goal of salvation, not faith.[26] The goal or end of sanctification is Christian perfection in love. God's gift of sanctifying grace is to restore that moral character of love that has been tarnished or perverted by the "Fall" of humanity.

The experience of God's saving and transforming love is a matter for the individual. It is a personal recognition and awareness of the need of and for God.

Transformation is also a communal act, however.

Wesley writes: *"[t]he gospel of Christ knows no religion, but social; no holiness but social holiness."* [27] In recognition of transformation as both an individual and communal process, Wesley devises a means for

---

[24] Ibid.
[25] Lindstrom, 102.
[26] See Deiter, 27.
[27] Maddox, 209.

such social and mutual accountability through "Christian conferencing."[28] Through Wesley's class meetings, band and select societies, people would gather to support one another in their active response of God's transforming work of saving grace. Both the Spirit of God and the worshipping community of which the person resides nurture the moral character of the individual. Love is not a truth to be held and discovered. Love is the life-affirming spirit that emerges as the result of relational living while restoring the corrupt moral image by and through God's love.

For Wesley, this understanding of God's power and love was contextualized within the culture of early Methodism through class rules and covenant groups.

The SMV reflects this understanding of salvation.

The Gospel and Southern Appalachia
The SMV is about contextualizing a Wesleyan perspective in a *hillbilly style.*

Many folk within southern Appalachia culture operate, socialize, and relate out of an oral culture. Though many everyday tasks require literacy, individuals cope, survive, succeed and fail and tell their stories and experiences amidst the use of proverbs and storytelling to convey and articulate

---

[28] Ibid.

opinions, ideas and accepted wisdoms. This is what Tex Sample labels as *"traditional orality."*[29] This culture is quite different from a "literary base culture" of dissertation, methodical rationality, and the discursive text.

Within an oral culture, philosophical and theological concepts are not construed and formulated by methodical and systematic reasoning. Many times such concepts are not expressed but are tacitly understood. Expressions come from the heart. This heart-language emerges out of empathy for others. Such expressions and experiences become crystallized as proverbs and used as metaphors in tell-able stories to communicate felt convictions that are unquestionably known to be true.

Relying upon the work of Walter Ong, Tex Sample's *"traditional orality"* is a way of talking about a culture that "knows" things that cannot be articulated, "feels" things that cannot be labeled, and "does" things that cannot be elucidated.[30] Ong makes a distinction between a *"primary oral culture"* and a *"secondary oral culture."* The former is a culture without a written language; whereas, the later is one that is literate but yet has a *"residual"* oral culture operating within it. Sample finds this label quite unfortunate because it tends to "demean" and thus

---

[29] See Sample, 3-12.
[30] Sample, 3.

to patronize: *"...to depict the concrete lived lives of people who manage to survive and cope--often being poor and near poor - and who do so with an endurance that would wilt and outpace most 'literate' people I know, and then call their culture 'residual,' is not only demeaning, it names something a 'leftover,' a 'remains,' a 'leavings,' that in fact, has as much permanence as writing itself. There is no literate culture without this 'residual' orality."* [31] For Sample, the term of *"traditional orality"* serves a better and more accurate nomenclature for a culture, which is quite literate in form, but yet quite oral in its function.

If southern Appalachian culture if one of orality, how then is the written word of Scripture expressed, transmitted and disseminated among the populous? Or put another way, how does the written word become part and parcel of everyday living that is much more informed by intuition and relational experience?

Ong suggests that the two questions imply and assume a community for determining meaning and definition: *"Written texts all have to be related somehow, directly or indirectly, to the world of sound, the natural habitat of language, to yield its meanings."* [32] So, within a culture that includes reading and writing, but whose appropriation and engagement are oral, how are and can the "good news" of a justifying,

---

[31] Ibid., 10.

[32] Walter Ong, *Orality & Literacy: The Technologizing of the Word*. (New York: Routledge, 1982), 8.

sanctifying, and liberating God be contexualized and appropriated? The answer once again is story.

By and with the use of proverbs and storytelling in the context of relationships that sustain and give meaning to the accepted wisdoms, faith language of traditional orality is *"expressively communicated [by means of both] sound and encoded language."* [33] Faith is much more of the "bosom" than it is of the "head" for traditional orality of southern Appalachia. If God's "good news" is found in the story of Jesus, how can it be expressively communicated in a southern Appalachian culture? The use of *"Jack Tales"* has been a prominent means of expressing that *"encoded language."*

Appalachian Jack Tales have their roots in the English, Scottish, Irish, German, French, African and Native American ancestries that populated the region of what is now called the Smoky Mountains. Jack was the "story magnet" for the floating folklore of a character that is sometimes portrayed as a fool or a laughingstock. He can also be characterized as clever, persevering, humble, or magical. Other tales depict him as a "trickster." [34]

In some tales, however, Jack takes on the attributes and personality of a *"shaman, culture hero, by*

---

[33] Ibid., 74-77.
[34] Donald Davis, *Southern Jack Tales*. (August House Publishers, Inc.: Little Rock, Arkansas, 1992), 13-14.

moving freely between natural and spiritual worlds, subduing evil, restoring harmony, and bringing blessings back to the community." [35]

This shaman and somewhat cultic hero is the Jesus of **The Gospel According to John Bill Bob Mark.**

He emerges from Newport, the cock-fighting capital east of the Mississippi; accompanied by the sarcastic suspicion, *"Can anything any good come out of Newport?"*

This *"Jack"* of a Jesus is captivating, alluring and repelling--depending upon which pole of the political and social magnet one may lean against. Just as the Jack of southern Appalachian tales was *"less of an individualized character than an emblem of human potential in many of its representative stages,"* [36] the SMV Jesus epitomizes a similar hope and promise.

The Jesus story of Mark is truly a narrative, a story. However, the purpose of the story is not to a make a point. Rather, the story of Jesus is the point. The use of story has been a common practice among all peoples to convey ideas and make points. Jack Tales do the same.

Jack Tales became effective, subversive and creative communications that expressed a dissatisfaction with the status quo and demonstrated a hope for change within a cultural of traditional

---
[35] Ibid., 14.
[36] Ibid., 15.

orality. The SMV of Mark is an attempt to speak of some of the same disappointments and hopes within the context of a Wesleyan Christian expression of southern Appalachia religiosity. It is both a telling of God's story and a community's commitment to that story.

Clarence Jordan's Cotton Patch Version is but one example of sharing the Christian faith from a perspective of "traditional orality." Jordan's use of the vernacular of the "southernese," in his words, was to *"help the reader have the same sense of participation [in the scriptures], which the early Christians must have had."* [37]

This SMV of Mark will be similar in style to the Cotton Patch Version, however, not in method. Whereas, Jordan was a New Testament scholar and translated from the Greek, I am not and I cannot. My work, at best, is a mixture of lexicon study and paraphrase from the New Revised Standard Version. Nonetheless, it includes more than that. In telling a good story, embellishment is both a southern Appalachian art and vice. I hope to be just as faithful to the text with an artful elaboration of the fantastic, moving, and empowering story of God.

This work will not be without its skeptics and critics.

Jordan also added that his approach was

---

[37] Clarence Jordan, *Cotton Patch Version of Luke and Acts*. (New Wine Publishing Inc.: Clinton, New Jersey, 1969), 7.

rather risky:

> The [Cotton Patch Version] may make the New Testament characters, particularly Jesus, too contemporary and therefore too human thus laying oneself open to charges of sacrilege and irreverence. Jesus has been so zealously worshipped, his deity so vehemently affirmed, his halo so brightly illumined, and his cross so beautifully polished that in the minds of [people] he no longer exists as a man. He has become an exquisite celestial being who momentarily and mistakenly lapsed into a painful involvement in the human scene, and then quite properly returned to his heavenly habitat. By thus glorifying him we more effectively rid ourselves of him than those who tried to do so by crudely crucifying him.
> Obviously this is not the thrust of the Bible. Its emphasis all the way throughout is on the humanity of God - Immanuel, God-with-us; upon incarnation - the word become flesh, here and now, in our experiences. Its movement is from heaven earthward, not vice-versa.
> So the 'cotton patch' version unashamedly takes the side of human beings rather than the angels.[38]

Jordan's honesty, courage, and audacity are both admirable and commendable.

Can this SMV be just as honest, courageous and bodacious to effectively communicate the "good news" of God? In the famous or infamous words of Patsy Cline about Kitty Well's singing ability, *"that ain't singin', bitch! That's whining."* For Cline, whining just doesn't come close to singing. Jordan attests that whining, holy or not, just is not God's way.

The SMV is about singing praises unto God who frees.

Here is the *"Word of God for the People of God"*--hillbilly style.

---

[38] Jordan, 7-8.

The Gospel According to John Bill Bob Mark
A SMOKY MOUNTAIN VERSION
BASED ON AND ADAPTED FROM THE GOSPEL OF MARK

HIT'S DRESSIN' UP TIME--THE COMMENCEMENT OF THE JESUS' PRACHIN'

(vs1:1)
A "Star" from the Beginnin'
It all commences with the good news of one of God's heavenly and earthly "stars,"[39] one of God's hillbillies,[40] Jesus the Christ, and 'hit all starts in God's country, the Great Smoky Mountains of southern Appalachia. Some have suggested these parts surely must belong to God because "no one but God would have it!"[41] That's only partially true.

---

[39] A "star" is a term of endearment. "After a spat, an old-time mountain man and bear hunter replied to his newly wed wife, 'You look like a star that fell from heaven, as she returned to him from her parents home." Cited from Joseph S. Hall, ed., *Sayings from Old Smoky: Some Traditional Phrases, Expressions, and Sentences Heard in The Great Smoky Mountains and Nearby Areas* (Asheville, North Carolina: The Cataloochee Press, 1972), 130. Subsequent references to this source are noted as *Sayings*.

[40] The term was "derogatory" in its initial use. It would not have been commonly used by mountain people but by "outsiders" to "socially locate." One of the earliest uses of the term was in the New York Journal of 1900, "A Hill-billie is a free and untrammeled white citizen of Alabama, who lives in the hills, has no means to speak of.....," *Sayings*, 85.

[41] *Sayings*, 74.

(1:2-13)
John Bob, the Baptizer

There was once a mountain prophetess who was born with a "veil over her face."[42]

She said, *"Lookie now and pay me some mind! God is sendin' a messenger ahead of the comin' goot news; this one will make ready for it's comin'. This rag-tag, bobtail mountain hoosier*[43] *will be cryin' out in the forgotten places of the ridges and hollers of these mountains; and he will be proclaimin': 'God's about to do somethin' special with these mountain folk! You just might think that they 'got no feder than Baker in the Blue Back Speller,'*[44] *but God done gone and proudly named 'em hillbillies!"*

And sure enough, John Bob the Baptizer appeared on Rich Mountain in Townsend, Tennessee of the Great Smoky Mountains.

Here, he was birthed and raised.

Just as the veiled prophetess had rightly seen, John Bob started proclaimin' a baptism that would lead 'em plumb[45] from one side to another - makin' 'em ready for the comin' of the goot news!

God's goot news is more than just a notion slap dab in the middle of the head. It claims hearts

---

[42] "The faculty of foreseeing future events is a well-known gift to those born with a caul, as well as a mark of good fortune and an ability to see and converse with ghosts....supernatural things....hidden from the eyes of ordinary [people]," *Sayings*, 138. A caul is the membrane that encloses a foetus or fetus.

[43] This is an old, dated and yet, derogatory term once used to describe rough or uncouth back country "white trash," see *Sayings*, 102-3.

[44] A common saying referring to the extent of one's education, see *Sayings*, 38.

[45] Completely, all the way, see *Sayings*, 109.

and changes 'em, too. For John Bob, puttin' on river water was the best attire for the arrival of the goot news.

People came from all around these parts. Even folk from Knoxvul[46] and Ashevul[47] made the journey! They all went upon Rich Mountain to see and hear what this rag-tag, bobtail, mountain hoosier had to say. They swarmed around him just like "yeller jackets in cotton blossoms."[48]

Brought to tears and moved by John Bob's words, people were baptized in the Little River at Kinzel Springs. Their tears could fill a gross of Mason jars, for they had stayed way too long in the "Devil's courthouse."[49] They pledged while God prepared their lives for the comin' of goot news. Each walked through those muddy waters from the north side of the river to the south.

Now, let me tell you about John Bob.

First of all, having two first names is as Southern as cheese grits.

Bob is short for Robert. It also reflected his character as a "bob-tail" mountain hoosier. Then, again, it may be because John Bob had always had a

---

[46] Knoxville, Tennessee.
[47] Asheville, North Carolina.
[48] *Sayings*, 144.
[49] A name given to "endless rhododendron tangles....[A friend told a neighbor that] 'he was going into the mountains to find his dogs or 'go to hell trying,'" *Sayings*, 58, 81. It is another way of talking about "hard times."

"likin'" for water--things usually "bob" in water, you know.

He is no fancy dresser. He wouldn't make a goot picture for the Sears and Roebuck catalog, that's for sure! Yet he was sure some kind of a "crackerjack."[50]

His entire wardrobe consisted of a pair of faded and worn Levi blue jeans, a wide black glossy leather belt with an oversized oval "Peterbilt" buckle made from bright silver pot-metal, a blue-gray flannel shirt (quite unlike cousin Lamar,[51] who liked red'ens), white tube socks, and a pair of dull black, but yet polished dingo boots.

He would eat whatever he could find, uproot or otherwise snare--which was just about anything. As a youngster, he was a good student about what and how to eat from the cupboard of the Great Smoky Mountains. His mama and grandma were even better teachers than he was a student.

While on Rich Mountain, John Bob said, *"There is one a comin' to bring God's goot news to these parts. I ain't worthy to be in the same company as he, much less strut in the same dance hall. I baptized you with this here river water, but he's a goin' to baptize you with God's water of new life from the rivers above!"*

As time and God would have it, there came a

---

[50] The constitution of a person is publicly defined by both choice of dress and attitude, see *Sayings*, 53.

[51] Wearing a red flannel shirt was a "signature" sign of Lamar Alexander's first Tennessee gubernatorial campaign.

fella by the name of Jesus, birthed and raised a young'in in Newport, Tennessee.[52]

Now as a man grown,[53] he came to give "ear"[54] to John Bob.

He, too, like many others was baptized in that mountain river. As he rose from the clingin' and cleansin' embrace of that swelled and muddied river water, the heavens done torn apart and the water of heaven's river spill't all over him.[55] Then a voice bellered and echoed through the ridges: *"You are my star, my beloved hillbilly!"*

The chill of both the river and heaven's waters sent Jesus to Townsend for some prayer and to "study"[56] about this God thang. With a warm heart, a clear head, and a soul "fit to be tied,"[57] Jesus found a night's lodgin' at the "Hillbilly Hilton."[58] There he prayed and studied on this new direction

---

[52] Newport is the unofficial "cock-fighting" capital of Tennessee.

[53] Jesus was a grown man, but the significance is much more than mere chronological age. "Man" also implies maturity and is an "earned" reputation. "When a man killed his neighbor's threatening bull out of self-defense, he went to the bull's owner and explained the details. 'If you hadn't come to me,' replied the 'bull-less' neighbor, I would always have thought hard of you. But you're acted a man, and I will too,'" see *Sayings*, 97-8.

[54] Listen.

[55] It's easy and hard to tell the difference between river water and heaven's water. Both will put a chill on you, but river water is dirty, unlike God's water. Besides, heaven's water warms your heart, clears your head and alters your direction.

[56] Think.

[57] Determined.

[58] No foolin'! There is such a place. It is located on the "main drag" of Townsend, Tennessee.

that God was givin' him. He studied and prayed a whole lot about the plight of God's hillbillies.

Jesus stayed in Townsend for forty days and forty nights. He was all alone except for the temptin' voices of the "Three-headed Religious Broadcasting Network," a.k.a., TBN, that blared its evil voice and cast its dark dull image on the bare wooden floor in an otherwise stark and empty room.

He didn't pay any mind nor heed to such things 'cause the peace and certainty of God and God's goot news was upon him.

(1:14-22)
Hit's Dressin' Up Time!

Months later, John Bob was handcuffed and hauled off to jail for *"inciting a riot and disturbing the peace,"* or so said the warrant, the rigged jury, and the sentencing judge. The truth, on the other hand, was as plain as trackin' a rabbit in the snow. He was supportin' and organizin' some textile workers at a local mill. John Bob was feisty and his bob-tail fur would "fly all over the place" when he got wind that some folks were mistreatin' a "lint head."[59]

Jesus, in the meantime, returned to his hometown of Newport, proclaimin' the goot news of God's kingdom a sayin', *"It's dressin' up time! Company's comin'! The kingdom of God is within earshot! It is within eyesight! God's agoin' to change the ways of this*

---
[59] Textile worker.

world like an old dirty shirt. Lookie now and pay God some mind!"

As he was travelin', Jesus passed along the French Broad River.

There, out of the corner of his eye, he spotted Shorty and his sister Evelyn Ann. Their clothes gave some clue about their lives. Dressed in worn, tattered, matching black jeans and soiled, darkened with sweat, white tee shirts, they were rummagin' for aluminum cans in the park trash cans near the river.

People called Shorty and Evelyn Ann poor.
Some called 'em shiftless and lazy.
"Redneck!"
"White trash!"
"Nigger!"
"Black trash!" are other names that came their way about as often as a bad day of huntin' for cans. Bad days was more than Shorty could count without getting naked!

On other occasions, the city folk just ignored 'em because they all noed[60] that hillbillies do nothing but "eat beef-jerky and stay drunk."

For the most part, Shorty and Evelyn Ann were "nobodies."

They looked like the "hind quarters of bad

---

[60] To be aware of, *Laughter,* 156.

luck."[61]

Searchin' for aluminum don't make you "preddy"[62] in the "mere"[63] of society, see? One just don't go to the university in Knoxvul to study the fine art of "Aluminum Procurement." There are a few days that paid-off in lookin' for cans, but for the most part, paydays were as few as honest politicians and short-winded preachers.

As for Evelyn Ann, she weighed in at about one hundred pounds when she was soakin' wet. Nearly half of her weight was "proud," at that.

This day was about to pay-off, but not in aluminum cans.

Jesus yaled[64] at 'em, *"I can show you a place where there are more cans than you can shake a stick at! Let's get all dressed up to go!"*

As strange as it may sound, they dropped their three days worth of collected aluminum cans and went with Jesus--all dressed up, sort of. The dressin' up had started in the hearts and minds of Shorty and Evelyn Ann. No need to tote around three days worth when there is a place that has more than you can shake a stick at!

As the dressed-up trio began their journey,

---

[61] See *Sayings*, 53-4.

[62] Pretty.

[63] Mirror, see Loyal Jones and Billy Edd Wheeler, *More Laughter in Appalachia: Southern Mountain Humor* (Little Rock: August House Publishers, Inc., 1995), 155. Subsequent references to this source will be noted as *Laughter*.

[64] Get the attention of another person.

they came to a boat dock on the lakeside. Jesus met Jimmy and Johnny, sons of Zeb, there. These two brothers managed and operated their daddy's boat marina.

Jesus axed[65] 'em, too, to come and join 'em. He axed 'em not because they was in need but 'cause they was needed.

So they did, leavin' behind 'em their father, the boat marina, and the hired hands.

Their walkin' 'den done took them to Dandridge.

They stayed there for a spell.[66]

When Sunday rolled around, Jesus went to the nearest church. While there he was axed to teach the morning lesson, so he did. Those present were astonished at his words and notions. However, it was his passion for God's forgotten people that turned their deaf ear.

Jesus convinced 'em that they were about to be freshly chiggered [67] in God's fields of love, hope, and freedom. They said that Jesus was different than most talkers.[68] *"Sure, there had been plenty of people that have tawlked about changes, but yet, those tawlkers*

---

[65] Ask, *Sayings*, 36-7.

[66] An indefinite period of time, *Sayings*, 129.

[67] A chigger is a mite in larval form that fastens to the skin, *Sayings*, 72. This "plight" is an outdoor phenomena! Therefore to be "freshly chiggered" is to be initiated into the wide-world of the fields with multiple little bites from the mites. In this case, the experience and acknowledgment of God's preventing grace is enough to get one "scratching."

[68] Talk, *Laughter*, 155.

peddled only half-hearted wishes and dead empty promises."

But not so with Jesus, or at least that's what some folks was sayin'.

(1:23-27)
A Change of Heart

Jesus was teachin' and a man with enormous wealth, but a cold heart, began shoutin' out from the back of the church, *"What have you to do with us, Jesus of Newport? Have you come to destroy life as we noed [69] it? Don't you noed that if people would simply get off their lazy pooossssteeeeeeerioooooors"* (he drew out the word for dramatic effect and continued) *"there would be no po' people! Po' people don't need anything except a big swift of kick of reality! Get real and get a life, Jesus! It's about time you built a bridge and got over it!"*

Everyone there noed this old-timer was "sot"[70] in his ways, except Jesus.

In turn, Jesus came back sayin', *"I hear the truth hammers a'poundin'! The truth of God's goot news will touch your heart, too, someday, if not sooner! Remember, life can take you in many directions, and it does!"*

Someone yaled out from the crowd,[71] *"That be right! Keep on prachin' Jesus! You prach while I pat my foot!"*

---

[69] *Sayings*, 81.
[70] Set, fixed, *Sayings*, 128.
[71] "How you get somebody's attention. You yale at them," *Laughter*, 155.

Sure enough, sooner came!

That man was touched!

That man became a willin' partner and accomplice of God's goot news! Right there in front of God and every body! His heart was warmed, his head started on its way to clearin'. He said that his spirit had been "bitten" and he knew that his life was "itching" for a new beginnin'. He was so moved by his experience that he "squawked liked a baby duck in a thunderstorm",[72]--just like the day that his mother gave him birth and breath. It was the first time since his childhood days that his heart could pour out its hurt and pain.

Yep, that unclean spirit of contempt and self-sufficiency left him that very minute. It left like "a scalded cat headin' fer a cat hole." [73]

Some of the people in the church was simply amazed at what they had just witnessed. They were amazed that Jesus was different from the "seminar"[74] professors who came through this way every now and then. Jesus used words that one didn't have to "give change for." You know, if you use a "twenty-dollar word" when a "nickel word" will get the job done, you gotta make change.

Others were shocked.

Many cried.

---

[72] A heart rendering cry, see *Sayings*, 63.

[73] In other words, fast! See *Sayings*, 61.

[74] Also known as "seminary," school for theological education.

They kept sayin' and a mumblin' amongst themselves, *"L-I-B!*[75] *I nary have seen a such! Jesus challenges even the cruelest and hardest of hearts and yet they crumble like cornbread!"*

(1:28-39)
In Need of More Than Just a Poultice
At once the words of love, freedom, and God's goot news began to spread throughout the surrounding region of the Smoky Mountains. Word done gone out that the Devil's Courthouse been taken over and got a new judge!

Jesus and his followers left the church and went to visit the kinfolk of Shorty and EvelynAnn.[76] Jimmy and Johnny were still taggin' along.

Shorty's aunt was burnt-up[77] with a high fever.

She had been told, *"you'd better git to bed, 'hit won't come to ya."*[78]

So she did.

Before goin' to bed, however, she made herself a mustard and onion poultice to fight it. She laid flat dab on her back and with a poultice on her chest for days 'cause she couldn't afford any doctorin'. When axed about how she was a doin',

---

[75] "Well, I'll be!" *Laughter*, 157.

[76] Aluminum can hunting can take one far away from home sometimes.

[77] A hyperbole, *Sayings*, 46.

[78] *Sayings*, 39.

she just replied, *"Me, ain't doing no good."* [79]

Someone told Jesus about her illness.

Jesus came to her bedside, kneeled and took her small, fragile but yet hardened and calloused hand; he then kissed it. Gently, he lifted her hand, gesturing for her to sit up slowly. Allowin' her to scoot over to the side of the bed, her danglin' feet nervously and anxiously searching for the floor beneath her, Jesus held onto her hand; he gently raised her hand, quietly and softly encouragin' her to stand.

As she took leave of the bed, the fever immediately left as well, with the poultice falling to the floor like a useless shoe in the summer time.

Everyone insisted on fixin' her some cooked cabbage and cornbread because she hadn't eaten in a long time.

So they did.

And she did!

After eatin' she said to 'em, *"By-cracky! You'uns just have a seat now. I'll whip up a fine sweet for dessert before you can say 'Jack Rabbit!'"*

And she did.

She was back to her old self.

That evenin', at the time of chickens roostin',[80] people brought to Jesus all who had

---

[79] *Do no good* means to be in poor health, *Sayings*, 60.

[80] That is, it is time to go to bed. This is the where the old saying,

poultices and couldn't afford any doctorin'.

Jesus did whatever and everythin' that he could do.

He talked to some.

For others, he offered to listen.

He remembered an old sayin' that his momma taught him long ago: *"Don't be talkin' when you ort to been listenin'--for a wise head keeps a closed mouth."* [81]

Some got an embrace.

Most importantly, he simply expressed God's love for and with them. He gave lovin' and understandin' to those who, at least in the eyes of some, were considered least deservin'.

That mornin,' but before the *"rooster crowed,"* [82] Jesus got up and went out to a small deserted cove of Douglas Lake made by TVA.[83] There he prayed and studied. He thought and prayed about the plight of God's hillbillies and how *"earthly hope could be just as present as heavenly hope."* [84]

While he was prayin', Shorty and his buddies, both new and old alike, was out huntin' for Jesus. They found him down in the cove. Shorty, short of breath and in a tizzy and all tore up, said, *"Dad gum it!* [85] *What are you doing out here? Everybody and their*

"Going to bed with the chickens," is derived.

[81] *Sayings,* 44, 135.

[82] Sign that hits time to git out of bed!

[83] Tennessee Valley Authority.

[84] *Sayings,* 64.

[85] *Sayings,* 54.

brother and sister is a' lookin' for ya!"

Jesus grinned and replied, *"Let's git on out of here! We need to yale God's goot news! We've got to be movin' on!"*

So they scattered throughout the Smoky Mountains proclaiming the message of love, freedom, and God's goot news in every church, in every house and in every place that would let 'em.

Jesus wanted to make sure that any and everyone noed about what God was a doin'.

Along the way, Jesus challenged God's critics, trippin' up their excuses.

(1:40-45)
God Loves Even Dram Drinkers

One day, an old dram drinker[86] came to Jesus and fell to the ground, clingin' tightly to the cuff of Jesus' rolled up jean pants.

He wept and begged, *"I know that you can hope[87] me! I know that you can hope me, if you choose! The corn[88] has done got a holt of me and hit won't let go!"* The depths of his cry would quicken any heart for it sounded like "a calf dying in hailstorm."[89]

Moved with compassion, Jesus stretched out his hand and touched the top of the man's head and said, *"I do choose. Be whole! God's love and freedom will*

---

[86] A drunkard, *Sayings*, 63.
[87] Help.
[88] Corn whiskey, *Sayings*, 51.
[89] *Sayings*, 46.

take holt in your heart."

Immediately the man's life was changed, or at least it started to change.

For the first time in a long time, however, he had self-respect. It was the first time that he had been able to hear that God's image was a part of hisself.

Now Jesus told him that change is evident only through time and added, *"See that you say nothin' to anyone; go home and go on expectin' and demandin' nothin' from anyone. Be committed to prove to yourself that God's love and freedom has found a home in your heart and your life. Fill your home with a graceful heart."*

The man, however, was so overjoyed that he went out and acted like he had been called to prachin' and told everyone about what Jesus had done. He would soon learn what really happened.

As a result of all this, life got rather hectic for Jesus. It was so hectic that he could no longer go out into the public openly without being axed for heaps[90] of hope of all sorts. He hid in the nooks and crannies of southeastern Jefferson County, but even there, people were able to find him.

Some demanded things.
Some had needs.
Others just wanted to talk.
Others needed to listen.

---

[90] Many, much, as in a great deal, *Sayings*, 79.

(2:1-13)
Junior Drives a Pick Up

After a few days, Jesus returned to Dandridge. People heard that he was a comin' their way again. Tongues and bell clappers[91] are the best modes of communication in between the hollers and ridges.

Quickly, they began to gather around Jesus.

People from all over collected at the small whitewashed and wooden-framed house where Jesus was found. The house was so slap-dad-full that it was like pouring ten pounds of mud in a five-pound poke.[92] Many others stood at the open windows hopin' to get a glimpse of Jesus and to hear what was on his mind and what he had studied.

Some folks from New Market, however, interrupted Jesus 'tawlkin'.

A man, on a home-made stretcher and bedridden for years as a result of an accident in a local zinc mine, was unloaded from the bed of an old dark blue Chevy pickup truck. They tried to carry the fella up into the house but the crowd of people on the porch was thicker than "six- hour old gravy." Seein' that they couldn't get through the crowd, they loaded him right back onto the truck bed.

Once situated, the driver kicked it into reverse

---

[91] *Sayings*, 137.
[92] A "poke" is a bag or sack.

and backed the truck right up onto the front porch with the folks scatterin' like "skeered chickens!"[93]

When Jesus heard the squawkin' and saw the commotion, he stopped in mid-sentence and made his way to the porch. Moved by the compassion and love of the stretcher-bound man's friends, Jesus said to him, all the while pointing to the four people who were sitting on the edge of the truck bed, *"You're mighty lucky, neighbor! Lots of people don't have neighbors like that!"*

"Most religious folks," Jesus added, maintaining eye contact with the bedridden man, *"let alone preachers, don't have near the compassion that these fine folks have shown today. They say that the amount of friends a person has is directly tied to one's willingness to forgive others. I reckon' you are a mighty fine forgivin' person."*

Some of those "seminar"[94] folk had gathered there too, 'cause Jesus had become some piece of work and a worthy subject for study. The thinkin' was that Jesus just might need some theological adjustment. One had suggested that if'n you followed what this here Jesus was stumpin', it's alikin' to *"climbin' to the top of a ladder and finding out that it's a'leanin' against the wrong wall."*[95] Now don't get me wrong, not all seminar professors are the same.

---

[93] Scared, afraid, *Sayings*, 119.
[94] That is, "Seminary."
[95] *Laughter*, 154.

They be some goot folk in the midst of 'em. It just so happened that this group gathered here was the sorriest of 'em all because they came with misdirected intentions not of their own makin'.

They were "sorry" because they were under the direction of the so-called ELITE.

The ELITE was made of the "dignified preachers" who let everyone noed of their "superior rank" as indicated by the multiple stripes on their elegant and dazzling multicolored flowing robes and television shows. For all practical purposes, these hand selected seminar professors had become the public eyes and ears for the ELITE. They had been told to *"git the scoop"* on this rabble that was *"pervertin' the faith, causin' too much trouble, and upsettin' the simple folk."* Besides, the ELITE informed the professors, *"This Jesus is becomin' as independent as a hog on ice,*[96] *and he needs to be corrected before he starts a messin' up a goot thing. Keep a keen eye on the fella."*

The ELITE was not too impressed with the folk that Jesus had made company. Their conclusion was that this here people was nothing short of being *"dirty, foul-mouthed, and just plain offensive!"* They further concluded that Jesus must not be any better, either.

"He ain't like any man of the cloth that I've ever seen or heard. I can't believe any God-fearin' person, let alone a preacher, would hang around and make company with that

---

[96] *Sayings,* 86.

level of rubbish, with stinkin' trash!" remarked one of the professors as he jotted down some notes in his spiral-bound memo pad. *"And besides,"* he continued. *"What's his authority for the things he did and does?"*

It didn't take Jesus very long to cipher[97] the real meaning for the gatherin' of these professors. So he turned to them and said, *"Howdy folks! Glad ya'll are here! By the way, can you imagine some crazy old fool drivin' a pickup truck right up onto this here porch?"*

Jesus got no reply.

Turning to the note-taker, Jesus continued, *"Such a fool must be one bad actor![98] Don't you think?"*

Still, no reply came.

Jesus wasn't lookin' fer a response by now and proceeded, *"What do you think is the easiest thing to say to a man stretched out in the bed of a Chevy pick-up? 'You're a lucky feller' or 'Git out of there and drive this thing home yourself?' So in order for you to know that God's power is as powerful as I have suggested, take a look see!"*

He turned to the man on the stretcher in the truck and said, *"Junior, git up from there and drive this truck off of this dad-jim porch."*[99]

Junior stood up!

Without help or assistance, Junior leaped from the truck bed, as quick as lightenin' but not as

---

[97] Discern.

[98] Reprobate, scoundrel, mean, malicious, deceitful, criminal, *Sayings*, 38.

[99] To this day no one knew how Jesus knew Junior's name. Of course, however, just about every other boy born in the south is called "Junior." Sometimes it is shortened to "Nooner."

dangerous. He jumped into the cab, turned the ignition key, put that sucker in drive, and drove off!

"Dad jimmit! Nary seen anything like this before," muttered a man from the "amen corner" of gathered professors, *"I'd better take note to this!"* His note said, *"I wouldn't believe it if I hadn't seen it myself. Hit would make my preacher lay down his'n Bible!"* [100]

After this, Jesus and his hillbillies returned to Douglas Lake; there people followed and gathered around him. He taught and shared the way of God's goot news.

(2:14-22)
Gene - A New Hillbilly

One day, during a break from his sharin' and teachin', Jesus strolled along the lakeside. Occasionally, he would stop to "skip" some flat rocks in the water, just like he had been taught years ago.

"Four, five, six, seven...eight! Not bad for a hillbilly," Jesus mumbled to himself as he counted the times the smooth dark stone skipped across the rather still blue-green crystal mirror of the lake's surface.

As he tossed another stone, he took notice of a man whose name was Gene. He was sittin' alone in a parked car at the TVA scenic lake park site. Jesus noticed right off that the car was government

---

[100] See *Sayings*, 102.

issue because of the green license plate.

Little did the world know of Gene's troubles.

No one knew exactly because Gene was too embarrassed to mention 'em to anyone. For him, however, his world was as "dead as four o'clock."[101] Gene was born into a family of complication, drama and pain; he was a typical southerner.[102]

Jesus approached the car and gently tapped upon the passenger's side front door window. Gene was startled by the repeated thuds that sounded like claps of thunder from without.

It was quite easy to read the pain on Gene's face.

Gene rolled down the window. Jesus poked in his head and said, *"Come let me show you a life of God's new beginnin's!"* It was Jesus' only greetin'.

So Gene let him! It was just that simple.

Later on in the day, Gene invited Jesus and the other hillbillies over to this house. There, Jesus kept company with many other southern hillbillies - many people that the world had forgotten or would rather forget.

Everyone was moved by the new possibilities which God's goot news was a'bringin'.

---

[101] Four o'clock in the morning is the hour when the restless dead cease walking and at four o'clock in the afternoon living people are "dead tired," see *Sayings*, 71.

[102] Many thanks to Pat Conroy for a succinct description of southern heritage. This description is found in his book *The Prince of Tides* (New York: Bantam Books, 1986), 109.

The professors, again, saw that Jesus was keepin' bad company. They said amongst 'demselves, *"Why does he keep company with such bad actors?"*

When Jesus heard this, he inquired of 'em, *"Now let me ask you this: Who needs family? Those with relatives or those without? God's goot news has done and come for those who see it and those who haven't seen it as of yet. God's goot news doesn't mean wishin' about it. It needs legs and feet, arms and hands, and hearts and souls; it needs lovin' people! Why when folks done git in the midst of this goot news, people will say that these hillbillies would just as soon play the fiddle and banjor and dance like billy goats.[103] When you hear the music, you can't keep from dancin'. Can you hear it? Celebrating sure is different than givin' up!"*

One day there was a religious rally led by the ELITE.

This was an excellent place for some political candidates to expound on the virtues of hard work and the merits of barbecuin' Spam on the grill.[104] Hit was also a goot time to get some bitchin' in about those folks who drain the economy of otherwise hard workin' folks like 'demselves. You could say at least one goot thing, or maybe two goot things, about these politicians. They were as cunnin'

---

[103] See *Sayings*, 41.
[104] *Laughter*, 162.

as a dead pig and only half as honest.[105] To support and justify their claims, readin's from the King James Version was consistently and constantly referred. The King James Version is the only recognized Bible amongst the ELITE. The reason, you ask? *"Why, Lord have mercy, child, that's the Bible that the Apostle Paul carried with him to Antioch. If'n it was good enough fer him, surely its good enough for God's people."* Or so they said.

Some of the professors came and inquired of Jesus: *"Why do some of John Bob's people and the good preachers read from the KJV of the Bible but your hillbillies don't even carry nary a one?"*

Jesus smiled and grinned like a possum.[106]

With the left corner of his mouth lifted ever so slightly above the right, he replied, *"Are words of hope and freedom restricted to the written page? Words on written pages have no life of their own; they just sit there until someone grabs them off of the page. The day has done come that these words have been grabbed off the pages and given a chance in the hearts of women and men who want and need it. I predict that some day, somewhere, some one will attempt to put them back on the pages. It is much safer that way. But until then, God is a'goin' to give life to God's hillbillies and both God and mountain folk know that 'you can't take no more on your head than you can kick off at your heels.'"* [107]

---

[105] *Sayings*, 107.
[106] If you look close, a possum wears a perpetual smile.
[107] *Laughter*, 165.

48

(2:23-28)
Silver Queen Corn and the Blue Laws

    One Sunday, a local farmer and would-be hillbilly told Jesus that he and his hillbillies could have an acre of his corn to sell at the farmer's market. The farmer said that this would be his way to help promote the message of God's goot news. The farmer didn't have anything else but his Silver Queen to give anyway. *"Besides,"* the farmer added, *"God has done gone and give me a goot crop, the corn's growin' so fast that you can hear the roots pop."* [108]

    Into the cornfield they went, picking the juicy, ripe, white ears of corn.

    Some of the ELITE, no one knows why they seem to stay in a pack, came to the edge of the field, watchin' and eyein' 'em real goot.

    One of the ELITE was elected to speak on behalf of the group.

    So he called to Jesus sayin', *"Look, why are ya'll doin' what is not right and lawful on a Sunday? Haven't you heard that the Sabbath is holy?!? And don't you know that you can't sell that corn today? Haven't you heard of the blue laws? We've worked awfully hard to keep people from buyin' things on Sunday. We've got to keep this day holy! So, why are you out here pluckin' dat dad-jim corn?"*

    While Jesus was being "blessed out" by this "dignified" preacher, a hillbilly started a fire to roast some ears to eat. It had been since yesterday

---

[108] *Sayings,* 51.

morning that anyone had eaten.

With the smell of roastin' ears floatin' in and out of his nostrils, Jesus replied to his accuser and the rest of the pack, *"Have you ever read about that David fellow in the goot book of yourin' and what he and his companions did when they was hungry and in dire need of vittles? It is right there in your black Bible. Well, that David fellow entered into the church house of God and ate the leftover cornbread from the altar. The pracher and the congregation was shocked to find that David had defiled that holy bread without eatin' it with buttermilk! Now that really fired 'em up!"*

With that Jesus walked away, carried away by the smell of the roastin' corn.

He then stopped, turned back to the pack and added, *"Dogs stay in packs because they are afraid of other dogs. Are you more afraid of what God can't do than what God can do? Let me remind you that Sundays was made for all folk, not the folk for the blue law Sundays. Remember people and God's goot news are fer more important than all of the blue laws of all Sundays!"*

Just when they thought Jesus was finished, he axed, *"Do you know where we can get some ramps* [109] *to go with this here corn?"*

---

[109] Ramp is a wild onion known for its pungent flavor, see *Sayings*, 113.

(3:1-5)
"That Sucker is as Goot as New!"
Later on and down along the French Broad River, Jesus visited another church. It was a Methodist church.[110] One of the faithful members of this small and intimate congregation was a man who had a maimed hand as the result of an accident in a rakin' machine. The man didn't have a "brownie to his name"[111] because of it.

Meanwhile, a couple supporters and backers of the ELITE, quite angry with Jesus by now, happened to be a part of this congregation and were present, as well. They watched in particular to see whether Jesus would offer to hope[112] this man on a Sunday. They had heard what happened in the cornfield. Anyway, they surely wished that Jesus would do somethin'! They sure were lookin' for a way to get him "fixed!"

Jesus took notice of the affliction of the man.

Jesus said to him, *"Come here my brother, you ole hillbilly."*

He did.

That's all it took, so it seemed.

The man's hand was fixed!

---

[110] A lot of people thought it was a funny thing that a Methodist church was located so close to so much water. *"That's probably why the church has so few members!"* some of the community residents would say under their breath but only while in the privacy of their homes. It is impolite to publicly talk about your neighbors.

[111] Money, brown, red, a cent pence, *Sayings*, 45.

[112] Help.

"That sucker is as goot as new!" exclaimed an observer in the midst of the congregation.

(3:6-7)
The Loyal Minority

Those two left the church and informed the members of the ELITE about what happened.

The ELITE began to scheme and plot with the Loyal Minority.[113]

Jesus had done exactly what they wanted, so now they could begin to "fix" him or at least somehow convince Jesus to tone down his rhetoric and to make sure that he wasn't *"leanin' his ladder the wrong way."*

Now, they really didn't want to hurt Jesus physically. They just thought that Jesus was out of line and was in dire need of some simple correction and tough love. *"Jesus was in need of an attitude adjustment,"* was the common rationale amongst the Loyal Minority. Besides, Jesus was causin' too much trouble for the goot people. *"It needs to be nipped in the bud, before it gits out of hand,"* came one determined suggestion from one who loved to watch the Andy Griffith Show.

Jesus left that Methodist church with his hillbillies in tow.

---

[113] The Loyal Minority was a religious/political group who saw their "God-ordained mission" to insure that everyone has a black KJV Bible in one hand and a pistol in the other. One just never knows when you might need one or the other, or so went the logic.

They returned to Douglas Lake with a few more hillbillies from the surroundin' mountain areas who had joined their number.

(3:8-13)
Telling the Goot News of Freedom
Hearin' all that Jesus was sayin' and doin', people came to him in great numbers from Knoxvul, Chattanoogie, Kingsport, Johnson City, and the Bristol area. When all these folks began to mix and mingle, a Knuxvillian, amazed by the discovery of a world beyond, was overheard to say, *"If the world's as big yan way, as it is yan way to Allegheny, my God, this world is a golly whopper!"* [114]

Word was getting out, mind ya!

As a huge crowd gathered, Jesus instructed a few of the hillbillies to have a jon boat ready for him at the dock. From the boat, he planned to share God's goot news of freedom.

By now, many had been challenged by Jesus' words and empowered by the embrace of the God who sent Jesus. Many came in order to hear God's goot news. In hearin' and being touched by the goot news, many would be able to begin to be more lovin' of 'demselves, forge their own history, and all the while openin' 'demselves to be the lovin' people that God had wished fer.

Many who had cold and indifferent hearts

---

[114] *Sayings*, 143.

were quickly changed and defrosted by the warmth and power of heaven's water.

One converted hillbilly said, *"I never really minded the fact that I had it so bad, but what pissed me off was that so many had it so goot."* Shoulder chips are soon forgotten when love and freedom have their way.

Many cried at their new found empowerment and freedom.

Others shouted.

A few wished to honor Jesus by worshippin' him.

Jesus told them, without any hesitatin', that they needed to be careful with their words.

"I didn't come to be worshipped," he responded and continued, *"I came to tell you about what God has in store for God's people. Don't confuse the two! Don't mock and make light of God's goot news with notions of bowin' and such!"*

He reminded them that there were people who resent what was a happenin' amongst 'em. *"They may try to hurt you,"* he added.

Jesus wasn't afraid of retribution by his di'senters. He did, on the other hand, fear for the safety of his sisters and brothers - the hillbillies. It was becoming quite clear that by simple association with him, people were at risk.

So, Jesus kept an eagle eye on 'em.

Jesus returned to the mountains and ascended

up to Clingman's Dome. There he spoke to those who were really interested in takin' part in the changin' power of God's goot news.

(3:14-20)
Commissionin' of the Goot News Hillbillies

From those who had gathered at Clingman's Dome, Jesus appointed and commissioned several women and several men to be God's hillbillies in both the proclamation and practice of goot news.

They was empowered to have the courage to challenge and cast aside the demons that oppress, impair and prohibit people from workin', livin', and lovin' together.

They could cast out the demons that kept people from knowin' and realizin' their own destiny and history.

They would be people of resistance.

They were devotees of Charley Pride, James Brown, Aretha Franklin, Merle Haggard, Patsy Cline, and yes, even Homer and Jethro.

On that mountain top these were the ones commissioned.

EvelynAnn.

Shorty--EvelynAnn's brother.[115]

Jimmy and his brother Johnny, a.k.a. Bubba -

---

[115] Jesus gave to Shorty the nickname of Junior. (Remember it is a southern thing.)

sons of Zeb, the marina owner.[116]
Phyllis from Riverdale.[117]
Along with Gene.[118]
Among 'em were some others:
Willie.
Jimmy Lee, the first born of Myrtle from Virginia and cousin of Pat.
"Backy."
D. Wood.
David and Mary K.
Staley, an ex-thespian.

Need not forget Pat, though some would like to do so, for he served as an undercover agent of SAM. He was also known as Johnny Ichabod.

Neither Pat nor SAM had the foggest notion about this Jesus thang.

After this, Jesus went home.

Now back in Newport, a huge crowd gathered.

I mean a huge crowd.[119]

(3:21-35)
Trash Talk!

By now, Jesus' family had become deeply

---

[116] To these, Jesus gave the nicknames of "Stink" and "Bait."

[117] You can take the woman out of the country, but you can't take the country out of the woman.

[118] Gene is sometimes called "Levi Gene."

[119] The "I" refers to the narrator's voice who often interjects thoughts and reflections within the story line.

troubled and worried about him. They had become upset for at least a couple of reasons.

First of all, a huge crowd gatherin' around your house makes for a whole lot of noise. Hit makes for angry neighbors. Being a good neighbor is an absolute requirement in the South and especially in the mountains!

The other reason was much more serious.

It is okay for family to talk about the shortcomin's of kinfolk. Family can say that *"his cheese done slid off his cracker"* without being hurtful or offensive. It's just a statement of fact.

It is different, however, when others, non-kin folk, start talkin' about your own flesh and blood. They can say *"bless his heart"* and still be respectful, but to say that Jesus must be *"at least a few pickles short of a jar"* would be totally unacceptable to family.

They began to hear other comments as well.

"He's two bricks shy of a load."
"Jesus is a bubble off plumb."
"He ain't got all his marbles."
"His marbles ain't rolling in the same groove."
"Jesus is as flaky as a bowl of Wheaties."
"He's long on drywall and short on studs."
"I don't believe his yeast rose."
"He's a forty watt bulb in a hundred watt world."
"Jesus is two dishes short of a picnic." [120]

---

[120] Adapted, *Laughter*, 160.

One lone voice vehemently proclaimed, *"Jesus is a communist from Highlander!"* [121]

You get the picture, right?

Kind of funny, right?

From the perspective of Jesus' kin, however, it was neither funny nor a laughin' matter.

First of all, it hurts to the bone to have folks talkin' about your kin. However, Jesus' family had been long infected with a terminal Southern disease of sellin' oneself short in life. Rumor has it that there is no vaccine fer it,[122] at least until now. Far too many of Jesus' blood line had died with it. Some kin felt like that Jesus may have gotten just a little above his raisin'. His family wanted to make sure that he not embarrass "mom an'em."[123]

Some of the professors that had come were still lookin' for ways to fix Jesus. They were still compilin' evidence to give a substantial and detailed report to the ELITE about Jesus' movin's about.

The professors decided they should and would take matters into their own hands. So they

---

[121] Highlander Folk School, founded by Myles Horton, originally located in Monteagle, Tennessee, and is now based in New Market, Tennessee. It has served and continues to be an education site for labor organizational skills, civil rights advocacy with the propose to educate *"for a revolution that would basically alter economic and political power relationships to the advantage of the poor and powerless...."* See Frank Adams with Myles Horton, *Unearthing Seeds of Fire: The Idea of Highlander* (Winston-Salem, North Carolina: John F. Blair, Publisher, 1975), 205.

[122] See Conroy, 469.

[123] "As when you're driving drive down the road, you see your neighbor, and you roll down the window and yell, 'How's your Mom an'em doin'?" *Laughter,* 156-7.

barged into the livin' room and began to set the record straight.

"Jesus, you've been actin' like the devil has got a holt on you. Here you are with all this scum and trash! You act like you ain't got a lick of sense. Where's your dignity, man? Besides, what's all this trash talkin' about anyway? We've been a thinkin.' Are you their leader? You must be because only scum and trash pay you any mind. Be forewarned that only evil can cast out evil."

By now, Jesus' family had left the house and stood in the yard, contemplatin' what went wrong with the once promisin' boy called Jesus.

"Now, how do you figure that?" Jesus axed in reply. "How can trash drive out trash? Can mud say to itself, 'Clean yourself up?' A family divided against itself is a family that's
a hurtin'. Right? And if a family is feudin' amongst itself, that family will be split right down the middle. Now ain't that right? And if the leader of trash raises up against other trash, ain't that leader on its way out, not in?

That's how I got it figured!

Besides, no one can go into SAM's house and take back what has been stolen without first SAM being tied up. Only then can people get back their stuff. I swear to all of you, that folk can be forgiven and freed of just about anything', but whoever thinks they are never in need of forgiveness or freedom, of course, never will. Even worse, however, hits a sin against God to take away and deny the opportunity for forgiveness and freedom."

Just then a spokesman for the professors jumped into the face of Jesus and screamed, *"Trash!"*
The spokesman noed SAM!
All this took place in that miniature living room of that small house. Hit was a hurtin' for "some elbow-room."[124]
Jesus' mother and the rest of the family came from the yard to the front porch and yaled for Jesus through the open window.
One of the folk sittin' around with Jesus heard the yalin' comin' through the window and said to Jesus, *"Your mamma wants you. She sounds like she means it."*
"Who is my mamma? And who is my kin?" Jesus axed in reply.
While lookin' at those who had found a home and the possibility of freedom and God's goot news in their lives, Jesus pointed to 'em and said, *"You are my mamma, too! You're my kin, too! For whoever walks God's hope, whoever talks God's goot news and whoever practices and lives both, they be my family!"*

---

[124] *Sayings*, 64.

Parables of Kingdom

(4:1-9)
The Poke With Dropsy!

Again, Jesus began to teach and share along Douglas Lake.

As usual, the crowd was so large that Jesus taught 'em from a jon boat so that the people could get an eye and ear of him.

Part of Jesus' popularity, if that is the right word, was that he taught differently than most. Instead of sermonizin' (most sermons include three points--whether there are three or not--and a poem, as needed, accordin' to some of the professors), Jesus spoke and taught from the everyday life experiences of everyday folk. Jesus found wisdom and insight in the stories of Jack, Minnie Pearl, Brer Rabbit, Lewis Grizzard, and Aunt Mae.

Jesus begun by sayin', *"Lookie now! It was spring time and the season for plantin'. A farmer went to the barn where he dried his seed durin' the winter. He had all kinds of seed in little two pound pokes. Little did the farmer know, however, that one of those pokes had the dropsy.*[125] *Hit couldn't holt onto anythin' because hit had a hole in hit. As he walked from the barn to the garden, some seed fell out. No need to worry about the fallen seed, the grey squirrels came by and et it up.*

Now, the seed that was not eaten, it just lay there on the well traveled beaten-down dirt path. When the roosters

---

[125] *Sayings*, 63.

crowed and the sun stretched its head and neck over the jagged mountain, the heat of the day scorched that fallen seed. Havin' no time and way to make root, that seed just gave up the ghost!

Some seed was caught by the afternoon breeze and tossed into the brush and thicket along the path. The seed eventually took root and shot straight up towards the beckonin' heavens. It, however, could not make crop because the brush and thicket choked it off from water and sunlight.

The seeds that didn't fall from the poke, the farmer planted 'em real good. 'Em seeds enjoyed sunshine, rain, nourishment, and care. The harvest was a goot one later. God helped, and so did the farmer. It takes both, you know."

Then Jesus concluded, "Now use your 20/20 ears!"

(4:9-23)
What's the Difference Between a Loaf of Bread and a Rhode Island Red?

Later that day, when Jesus was alone, many came to him and axed him about the meanin' of his parables and stories.

"Now, I thought that ya'll had a clue about what God's freedom and goot news is all about. There are plenty out there who don't have a clue, but surely you do!?" Jesus inquisitively responded.

"Now let me ax you somethin'," he added. "If just plain smartness is the key to knowin' God and God's goot news, 'den answer me this question. What is the difference between a loaf of bread and a Rhode Island Red?"

    As the inquirers scratched their puzzled heads providin' no reply, Jesus followed with another question, *"Do you not remember the story I told on the lake about the poke with a hole in it? If you don't understand that one, how about all the others I told? Let me try to explain...The farmer is like a hillbilly proclaimin' and livin' the message of God's goot news. It's also about SAM.*

    The farmer plans to plant those seeds in the 'bestest' of places.

    Some don't get planted, though.

    Some fall on hard, beaten down ears.

    There are some people who just don't really care about folks like hillbillies. Some people just would rather forget and ignore white, black, and red trash. And since this word of goot news falls on ground that has no heart, it ain't going to make seed and root. SAM is still doin' SAM's thang!

    For some other folks, this hope is nothin' more than squirrel food.

    For the seed that was eaten by the squirrels, it is like people who hear and receive God's freedom with joy. But soon afterwards they realize that this seed demanded somethin' from 'em that they can't give back. They might have to weed, till the soil, mend a fence, or clean a fence-row. Hope and freedom just seems like too much trouble; they would prefer that things just stay the same. The sun of indifference eventually dries up that joy. SAM is still at it!

    And for the seed that was blown into the brush and thicket, it is the same for those who hear and receive the goot news, but temptations of cable television, expensive cars, back yard swimmin' pools, and life at the country club are just far more important. Sure, you can obey all the commandments but yet still not care a lick for others. These folks sure do look like goot plants, but they never make a crop of hope and freedom. SAM is still at it and SAM is still the MAN!

You tawlk of makin' good crop, that's the seed planted by the farmer in the garden. They hear the goot news of God's love and freedom, receive it with joy and live it!"

"Besides," Jesus continued in conclusion. "Does anyone wire a house just to stay in darkness? For those things that appear to be hidden and secret can be found and seen with the flip of a switch!

What is the difference between a loaf of bread and a Rhode Island Red? 'Cause if'n ya'll don't know the difference, I'll never send you to fetch a loaf of bread!

Now use your 20/20 ears!"

(4:24-29)
You Get What You Put Into It!

Jesus wasn't finished. *"A worker is worth a just wage. So pay careful attention to what your ears hear and your heart feels; remember that you get what you put into it.*

For those who commit to more, surely more will be available. For those who put nothin' into it should expect exactly that! And listen and know this: God's freedom and goot news is like a farmer plantin' a mater [126] *seed.*

Once the seed is in the ground, there is nothin' yet to

---

[126] Tomato.

do. Just eat, sleep, and cut mater sticks. You don't know why the seed germinates, it just does. The ground, the seed, and God just work together.

In due time, the ground produces a seedlin', then a stalk. Then you stake it. It blooms, and then comes the 'mater.

When the 'mater is ripe, you pick it.

You slice it and make a 'mater and mayonnaise sandwich. There ain't anything hardly any better! But what kind of sandwich is you left with if you never plant the 'mater seed?

You git what you put into it!"

(4:30-36)
Freedom is Like an Apple Seed

Jesus also said, *"There are many ways of understandin' God's freein' us up. It is like the seed of an apple. It is small in comparison to a pumpkin seed, yet when that apple seed is planted and takes root, breaks the ground and begins to stalk, it grows big enough to bear fruit and provide a home to be fancied by the loneliest of birds. The apple seed becomes a tree that is both a eatin' and sleepin' place!"*

With many such parables and stories and the like, Jesus spoke the words of God's freedom with 'em. It was up to 'em as to the real meanin' and if the meanin' was real.

He always taught with such simple ways, but to those who didn't have 20/20 hearing and wanted to know more, Jesus went the extra mile to help 'em along.

As evenin' came, Jesus insisted, *"Lets go across to the other side."*

So they did.

Some just took Jesus at face value about going to the other side--to the other side of the lake, that is. I wonder if Jesus had something else in mind, too?

Leavin' the huge crowd behind, Mary and David K. jumped into the boat with Jesus. Other boats followed.

MIRACLES AROUND DOUGLAS LAKE
(4:37-41)
Shorty Forgets His Short Wave Radio

Havin' paid no mind to the loomin' thunderstorm in the sky above, Shorty was caught off guard by a storm gale that quickly brewed. The prospect of tunin' to the National Weather Band was not an option. Shorty had left his radio with his cart of aluminum cans when he first met Jesus.

Quickly a thunderstorm and gale wind fell upon the lake like a heavy hand stitched quilt. Momentarily hoverin' above the bed of the chopping waters, the storm fell with a deafenin' thuuuuuuudddddddd!

Hit come a storm!

The waves began to bark loudly and violently snap at the sides of the boats just like a old stray dog givin' chase to a cow in the pasture.

However, Jesus remained calmly seated in the rear of the boat, seemin' asleep and payin' no mind to the noise and violence that now invaded the once tranquil lake.

David K. shook Jesus and said, *"Hey Jesus, what in the livin' daylights are you doin'? Don't you give a rat's tail that we are all about to either be fried by the lightnin' or swallowed up by these lappin' waves?"* David K. then turned his attention to the others in another boat and yaled, *"Who in the name of Jimmy Dickens put this dog in this here boat? We'll sure be fried crispier than*

KFC chicken tenders!" [127]

Jesus stood up in the jon boat and rebuked the wind, scolded the lightnin' and instructed the lake water, *"Rest, my sister, rest!"*

The wind stopped and a soothin' calm returned.

Jesus then turned and said to 'em, *"You haven't seen a real storm yet! Have you faith in God's goot news?"*

The two were amazed by Jesus' courage.

They could not believe that words could be so powerful.

They couldn't believe that words could soothe the wind and tame the lake. Well, not until then, anyway.

(5:1-20)
A White Capped Bubba

They arrived on the other side of the lake in Sevier County.

As Jesus stepped out of the boat, a man ran up to him.

(Watch out! Another storm is brewin'!)

This man looked just like any other except for the white cap that was coned upon his head. The white-capped man lived alone in the mountains, outside of Gatlinburg. He was a rather smart fella

---

[127] It is a well known thought in the mountains that a dog will attract lightning. Many a folk have been known to drive hounds away from their cabins during a storm with the notion that a "dog's tail draws lightnin'," see *Sayings*, 62.

and a better tawlker. He had gotten all the way to "Zebra" in the Blue Back Speller and could argue that a cow patty was apple butter! However, when the white cap was donned upon his head, it seemed to have a mystical power of rancor, hate, and bigotry all over him.

A bigot with a white cap! Imagine that!

No one could match his wit and tongue, not even the folks from UTK![128] Even those who were in agreement with his racial philosophies found him to be a pain in the neck, but others, their opinion of him was much lower.

Night and day, this man ranted and raved, discussed and cussed about foreigners, poor folk, and others that found 'demselves on the margins of life. Night and day, as long as he wore that mystical cap, he was found tossin' the stones of bigotry and hatred at anyone who was different from hisself.

(That's enough about him; let's return to the lake.)

Strangely enough, as Jesus jumped from the boat, this man ran in pursuit of him like a hound after a raccoon and yaled at the top of his lungs: *"What have you to do with us white trash here? Don't come a botherin' us with your 'love your neighbor' baloney. We hear it all the time! We hear it from the people that put the screws to us!"*

(I did warn ya about a pendin' storm. Did

---

[128] The University of Tennessee, Knoxville.

you hear the thuuuuuuudddddddd?)

Jesus smiled and replied, *"Yep, you're right...So I won't say it."*

And then it happened.

The winds stopped.

For some reason that was unexplained, at least from this distance, there was somethin' that had been implanted into that fella's heart just like that goot seed that the farmer planted real deep in the goot soil!

That fella snatched the coned white cap right off of his own head and threw it onto the lake's muddy shore! He began to stomp, grindin' hit into the soft and shallow, dark, brown muddy ground beneath the sole of his worn but polished black dingo boots.

Jesus, watchin' the transformation before him, inquired, *"You seem to know my name. What's yours? What does your mamma call you?"*

"Bubba."

"Are there many white capped Bubbas around?" Jesus wanted to know.

"Many."

Bubba was becomin' part of God's freedom and goot news. He stood there, humbled and troubled, with his cap still beneath his right foot, drownin' in the lake's water.

Jesus understandin' and acceptance humbled him.

Bubba was troubled with his past.

"*What can I do with it?*" he prayed silently.

Not far from the landin' area, there was a pig farm. Everyone knew about it because the nose just won't lie! Bubba repeated his short and contrite prayer again with 'hit becomin' louder and somewhat directed towards Jesus.

Jesus overheard him and then suggested, "*What if ya throw it in one of those pig pens? I don't think the hogs will mind. They'll either ignore it or trample it under their feet. It will eventually be buried. Hatred needs to be buried. Don't you think?*"

So Bubba did.

And some other Bubbas and Bubbaettes did as well.

In just a short time that pig-pen looked like it had been covered with a velvet white layer of frosty winter snow. Just as quickly as the hoods appeared on the pen's floor of muck and manure, however, they all disappeared under the indifferent and mud-caked feet of the pigs, a proper burial with a pendin' and proper resurrection.

The pig farmer, however, thought differently.

He ran to get assistance from the authorities for the intrusion onto his property. They arrived with the farmer, findin' Jesus and Bubba sittin' and quietly tawlkin'. They didn't know what to make of it all. Bubba had a pretty good reputation for "shootin' off the jaw," but yet now he seemed so calm, peaceful.

The witnesses from the boats and others that had gathered became fearful that other powerful white caps, though not all wear the caps in public, might seek revenge against this intrusion started by Jesus.

Jesus was told to move on.

He agreed to leave.

Climbin' into the boat, Bubba begged to go with Jesus.

"Nah," Jesus charged him. *"You go home to your friends and tell them about God's freedom. You tell them of what God is a plantin' and that God is in the midst of a raisin'!"*

So Bubba did.

Bubba went to preachin', witnessin' and testifyin' to a new freedom experienced from God. Hit had begun to change him. Everybody, I mean everybody, includin' their own brother and sister, was amazed at the new emergin' Bubba.

(5:21-43)
A Family Crest

As Jesus crossed to the other side, he was greeted by another huge crowd, right there, smack dab on the lake.

A church leader, Jeremiah, called Jerry by his family and from a small country church in Jonesborough, saw Jesus. He came and fell at the

Jesus' feet, weepin'.

Sobbin' uncontrollably, he managed to give words and voice for a heart that was breakin', *"My daughter...My little daughter.... is dying! Can you hope her? Please hope! I have no other place or person to turn to! Will you...."* His words gave way to the more powerful sobs of despair, hopelessness, and resignation.

"Yes," came the gentle and assurin' reply from Jesus. *"Let's go."*

Jesus began to walk with Jerry close to his side.

They were walkin' in a hurry.

The huge crowd tried to keep step and in stride with 'em.

The crowd pressed inward, close to Jesus. In the midst of the crowd, in the middle of the pushin' and polite shovin', was a woman who was sick and disfigured from a painful and cruel ailment.

She had visited every doctor around. Though each doctor did their darnest, she remained ill. After all the visits, however, came all the bills.

By now, she was a woman with no health, and no health care.

No money.
Disfigured.
Sick.
Homeless.
And it all started with so-called managed care.
This was her life.

This had been her life for the past twelve years.

The thirteenth year looked no different.

Once through an open window of a small house, she had heard Jesus' invitation to be a part of a new family. Her sickness had separated her from her kin and removed her from loved ones and even friends. She had a deep-seeded need to belong, to belong to someone and to feel that she had a space where that belonging could take place.

I suspect that was the reason she had the courage to do what she did next.

So in the midst of the crowd she reached toward Jesus, desperately tryin' to touch or even grasp the family crest that Jesus wore on his blue and gray flannel shirt pocket.

As she reached, graspin' now only the thin spring air, she muttered to herself, *"If I but touch that crest, I, too, will be part of Jesus' family. What have I to lose?"*

She finally traded her grasp of summer air for a momentary, but yet firm holt on the crest.

The mere touchin' brought memory of strength!

Images of family faces and friends' places.
Faces of people long missed.
Places of belonging.
Places of being needed.
And wholeness!

Echoes of being called by her name.
Jesus stopped.
Her grasp was quickly broken.
"Who grabbed me? Who touched me?" Jesus demanded to know. *"Who grabbed me by my family crest?"* pointin' and gesturin' to his shirt pocket.

Gene spoke first. *"Come on, Jesus. How in the world could you ask 'Who?' It's like searchin' for a minnow in the middle of Douglas Lake. There is enough people around here to have a Lodge convention."*

Jesus, however, continued to survey the crowd without respondin' to Gene's commentary.

The woman who touched Jesus was now both afraid and ecstatic.

Terrified, she knew the feelin' of public humiliation and mockery; it was an every day experience. *"What if he resents me touchin' him,"* she said under her breath, adding, *"I'm afraid others might agree and not like it either."*

"Something is different," as she continued to speak to her mind's ear. She was listenin' with her 20/20 ears. *"I do, on the other hand, feel like I belong! I feel like I belong to his new family!"*

She politely, but hurriedly, approached Jesus and spoke somewhat softly and reluctantly, *"I touched...."*

Words of pain and humiliation are often hard to voice.

"I did. I touched you....I meant no harm....But I've

heard you say...."

Before she had the opportunity to finish, Jesus said to her, *"My sister! My sister, JennySue, I've been lookin' all over this country and mountainside for you. I'm so glad you're home. God gave you the courage. God has done claimed and got holt of you!"*

As Jesus spoke, a cousin of Jerry came and whispered sadly into Jerry's ear, *"Your daughter is gone. No need to bother Jesus. But if that old witch hadn't gotten in the way,"* pointin' to the frail woman and finished, *"Jesus would have been at your house by now!"*

The words of death caught the earshot of Jesus.

He kissed the forehead of the woman, then approached and embraced Jerry, whisperin', *"The best of all is, God is with us."* [129]

After these words, Jesus instructed that only Shorty, EvelynAnn, Jimmy, and Johnny would make the walk to Jerry's house.

They came to the small but well-kept three-room dwellin'.

Relatives and neighbors had already gathered to make preparations for the wake. The place had the feel of unanswered prayers and the smell of fresh flowers. Preparin' for death, instead of plannin' for life, seems a rather cruel act. Life was

---

[129] This is attributed to John Wesley as his final "statement of faith," see Richard P. Heitzenrater, *Wesley and the People Called Methodist* (Nashville, Tennessee: Abingdon Press, 1995), 308.

just gettin' started for this young woman-to-be. The endin' of life should be reserved for those who have chased their dreams, who have been given the chance to love, and be loved, or so it is said. Death is a cruel mockery of life when hit visits the young. But this is all too common here in the mountains.

Jesus grieved for and with the mamma and daddy.

He then said the rather absurd.

"Please don't be afraid. She is merely sleepin'!"

Many saw the absurdity and scolded Jesus, *"Don't be cruel. It is enough that this has happened to 'em, their only child. Don't make it worse by trivializin' with religious cliches. Don't give 'em false and shallow hopes."*

Jesus understood.

Jesus took the father with one hand and the mother with the other and led both of 'em to the bedside of the child. They knelt down beside the bed that for the moment served as an open casket for a dead child.

Jesus prayed.

He then took the child by the hand, stood up, and proclaimed, *"It's dressin' up time, little darlin'."*

There before the startled but delighted eyes of her mamma and daddy, the child sat up in the bed, rubbin' her eyes as though greeted by the mornin' sun after a long winter's night sleep.

She would be able to celebrate her thirteenth birthday.

The cryin' continued, but now the tears were ones of joy.

The parents embraced each other. They hugged their daughter and then Jesus. They offered their farm as payment for his services. Jesus refused by sayin', *"Miracles are everyday. We just don't take the time to see and enjoy them. Now don't make this child a public oddity by havin' her appear on Oprah or Jerry. Don't broadcast this! Just continue to love and nurture her. I'm sure she may be hungry for some scrambled eggs and cheese grits."*

MORE PRACHIN' BY JESUS

(6:1-6)
Sunday Prachin'

Jesus left and went to Newport, his hometown, with many of his hillbillies in tow. On this Sunday, he prached about God's freedom with wisdom, insight and passion. Many who heard him were amazed and bewildered. They said among 'emselves, *"Where did this fella get all this? Where in the name of UTK did he get all these smarts? Wherever he got it, look how it has affected other folk. But isn't this the millwright, the son of MaryJane and brother of Jimmy, BobbyJoe, Justin, Sammy, and aren't his sisters SallieJane, Beulah, and Millie here with us too?"*

The more they thought about it all, the more they were convinced that Jesus was beginnin' to act just a little bit uppity and talkin' above his raisin'.

"He's getting above his raisin'!" seemed to be the general sentiment.

(See, I told ya.)

Now, the more they thought about it, the madder they got. They were as *"ill as hornets."* [130]

Jesus ignored their snipes and attempted stings addressin' 'em by sayin', *"Those who speak and spread God's power receive respect from just about anyone and every where, except in their own holler, among their own kin, even among those who noed and loved 'em the best."*

Realizin' that there were no willin' ears to

---

[130] *Sayings*, 88-9.

listen for the goot news, no willin' hands to cradle it, and no willin' hearts to allow it to call home, Jesus just didn't say or do much more there, except be with those who are sick and with those searchin' for new and whole lives.

The lack of interest and stake in God's power disturbed Jesus.

So he left and went to the surroundin' mountainside, prachin' and teachin'.

(6:7-14)
The Tradition of the Walking Stick

One day Jesus called some of his hillbillies and talked with 'em about spreadin' out to share the message of the goot news of God's freedom. Those who chose to go, he sent 'em in pairs, encouragin' them to have the gall to challenge the Devil's Courtroom.

He reminded 'em of SAM!

Jesus prepared 'em for the journey.

"Carry nary a walkin' stick. Nutin' else should be in y'all's possession that might hinder the way. Yourin' dress should be simple, dingo boots, blue jeans, and tee-shirts, and no jackets without union labels."

Jesus further added, *"Now when you are invited into a house, be a goot guest. Show goot manners. Be polite. Don't think that they are there to serve ya. Be strong and consistent in word and deed. Make sure your words are ones of God's hope, lovin' power, powerful love and freedom, not vengeance and hatred. Don't be flighty. If a person opens up his'in or her'in home to God's freedom, embrace your new and long lost family and call 'em by name!*

If any place or anybody won't welcome ya and refuses the freedom offered by God, don't fret, and I'm not talking guitars here, just count it as their loss and move on. Don't even take the dust of that place with you. Shake it off!"

So they went.

In pairs they prached, teachin' and practicin' being lovin' hillbillies of God. Great things began to happen in the lives of folk who had lived so long resigned to being "sick-and-tired of being sick-and-tired." You couldn't imagine the changes that came about. Even the commissioned hillbillies were amazed.

"I guess this is really true!" one hillbilly confessed to another.

Now Governor Pardon, a powerful broker of political favors, heard what Jesus and his hillbillies was a'doin'. One of his advisors suggested that John Bob, the Baptizer, had come back from the dead.

"Yep, that explains it all," sassied the wisest of the governor's advisors.

(6:15-31)
Myles Horton or Nostradamus

There was another advisor, sharper than a well-dress hand ax, suggested something else. *"No! No, ya'll got it all wrong. John Bob ain't come back! It must be Myles Horton, that communist!"* Another offered a less political explanation, *"You are both wrong! This Jesus is a prophet like Nostradamus."*

Governor Pardon, however, was not satisfied with any of the explanations and replied, *"He must be John Bob reincarnated. I thought that we had gotten rid of that SOB and all the SOBin' trouble that he stirred up. Yep! John Bob has come back and I noed that to be gospel because I saw such a thing on Oprah! Besides, when I saw Elvis at Wal-Mart yesterday, he done told me it was so! That's proof enough!"*

Remember now, it was Governor Pardon that sent the state police to Newport to arrest John Bob. John Bob was handcuffed and imprisoned for supportin' and organizin' the "lint heads" at a local mill. John Bob died in the state penitentiary in Nashville at the hands of some inside paid cronies. That's what is called "effective politics!"

Now don't get me wrong.

John Bob was guilty all right.

He was guilty of sayin', *"It ain't right! It ain't right that these people be treated this way--low wages, no benefits, no insurance, long hours, and an unhealthy and unsafe work place."*

Norma Jean's mother was one of the first to sign up for the union.

The mill owners took all this kind of personal and wanted to get shed of John Bob and all of that union tawlk. They couldn't do it by themselves, but they tried.

The Governor was asked to intervene on the behalf of common sense and the free market. However, the Governor respected John Bob as a great spiritual man. As a matter of fact, Governor Pardon thought that John Bob was on to somethin'.

So when John Bob spoke, he listened.

He listened even to the troublin' words that were troublesome to a troubled heart.

The opportunity, however, that led to John Bob's death came when the Governor celebrated his sixtieth birthday on the lawn of the state's mansion.

State leaders and famous people from all around came to join the festivities.

Now a dancer from the "Mouse's Foot," a local dancin' club and bar, had been hired by his brother to perform and sing "Happy Birthday" for the Governor. His brother had his hand in the financial "cookie jar" of textiles in Appalachia. He knew that his brother, the governor, had a weakness for whiskey and dancing women.

The Governor was so pleased with the attention during the day, he said to the young dancer, *"Whatever your little heart desires, I'll git it fer ya."* By now, the whiskey was tawlkin' for the Governor.

The Governor stood with his right hand across his chest and swore, *"Now, young lady, I mean every last word that I am about to say. Why, shucks, if you were to ask for half of this state, I believe I'd git it fer ya."*

The dancer went to the governor's brother and said, *"It's your call, now."*

She rushed back to the Governor and whispered, *"I don't want nothin' much. I just want John Bob. I don't want him ruinin' jobs for my family back home. Just let your brother take care of the whole situation. Let him fix things!"*

Governor Pardon noed how his brother "fixed" things. He was troubled by the request but gave in to it because he swore before all those people. Nobody likes a politician that don't keep his or her word!

It was a done deal.

Word was sent to the state prison that somehow and somewhere, John Bob was to die. It didn't matter how.

"Just make it look like an accident!" was the only instruction.

Within hours and by late evenin', word was received that John Bob was dead.

Bone dead!

John Bob had accidentally fallen in the shower with his skull split wide open. He died before a doctor could see him.

John Bob was given proper burial and respect by some of his followers. No one, however, really believed the report that it was an accident caused by a slip on shower soap.

When the commissioned hillbilly pairs returned later, they gathered around Jesus and told him all that they had seen, done and witnessed, all in the name of a lovin' God and God's power!

Jesus affirmed their witness by sayin', *"Mighty fine! Mighty fine! Excellent work! Let's get away for awhile."*

All of 'em, includin' Jesus, was tired.

(6:32-44)
Service with a Smile and Faster Than Mickey D's

So they went by boat to a secret cove somewhere on Douglas Lake.

(If I noed exactly where they went, it wouldn't be a secret, now would it?)

However, so many people did find out and gathered around the shoreline to greet 'em.

As Jesus climbed out of the boat, he was overwhelmed by the vastness of the crowd. The vastness was not just in the size. It was the vastness of the people's history whose whole past, identity, and personhood had been suppressed, ignored, and neglected. He decided it was more important to stay with 'em than to journey onward.

Jesus and his hillbillies tawlked and shared late into the evenin'.

One hillbilly came to Jesus and suggested, *"It's about time for the chickens to roost.*[131] *We better get to the*

---

[131] Time to go to bed and sleep.

cove so that these people can leave. Besides, it's almost late and they don't need to be out here. They need to be at home. We haven't even eaten supper yet, anyway. I'm quite sure that they must be starvin' too! Backbone to belly button, I bet! Why don't we just send 'em home, so they can eat. There are plenty of places they can go, but there ain't no place here."

Jesus grinned and replied, *"Let's feed 'em!"*

"Yeah, right, Jesus!" came a retort. "We'll just take all the money that we didn't make in the past year and we'll march down to Mickey D's and get enough to feed all these here people. And when we are axed to pay for it, we'll just say we are waitin' for our rich uncle and aunt to get out of the poor house!"

"That be right!" echoed a voice from the amen corner.

Jesus was impressed with the humor but was disturbed by the lack of compassion. So he inquired, *"What food do we have with us? Someone check. Now!"*

Just as quick as Gene left to find out, he returned with a very short list of rations. He read the list with a sheepish grin on his face,

"Well...We've got five loaves of Sunbeam bread.

A jar of fat-free mayo.

A packet of mustard.

Two cans of sardines and a stale, green-looking Twinkie."

And then added, but not too loudly, "Yep, that will just about take care of a few thousands of folks...."

Without hesitatin', Jesus ordered the hillbillies to organize the folk in small groups and have them sit on the green grass that separated the lakeshore and the road behind it.

So they did, not knowin' nor askin' why.

And the people sat.

Takin' all the provisions Gene found, includin' the green Twinkie, Jesus looked upward towards the heavens and thanked God for the mess. He opened the loaves of bread and the cans of sardines and started to hand them out.

And strangely enough, all ate.

Everyone ate and was filled.

Those who ate that day numbered about five thousand.

(6:45-56)
Light Struck Possums

Follown' the meal and after dismissin' the thousands, Jesus told his hillbillies to get back into their boats and head to the secret cove.

Jesus stayed, however, and went to a nearby hilltop to pray, alone. Later, as Jesus viewed the boats castin' their shadows against "mere" of the waters created by the full moon's light, a sudden thunderstorm moved in. The thunder rumbled, the winds howled, and waves began to snap up against the jon boats. Hit was comin' a storm! Seein' the hillbillies in trouble, Jesus descended from the hilltop and began to walk in their direction, right on top of the water, mind ya!

When they first saw him, however, they mistook him for a haint.[132] They were so frightened that they moved not one muscle. They looked and acted like possums paralyzed by a bright light that intrudes on the tranquility of a dark peaceful night.

Jesus reassured 'em all, *"Don't fret. It's me!"*

He climbed into the nearest boat.

The thunder stopped, the winds ceased and the water become calm. Those in the boats were speechless. How do you explain somethin' that you wouldn't and couldn't believe unless you seen it with your own two wide-open possum eyes?

They were still tryin' to figure out the feedin' of the thousands, and now this!

They made their way to the cove and tied up their boats.

Little did they know that the secret cove was no longer a secret.

As they landed, once again, they were greeted with folk from all around. From there, they followed the hillbillies to New Market.

There at New Market, more people rushed in bringin' their hurts, needs, and sick with 'em. It didn't matter where Jesus found himself, people and huge crowds at that, found him.

And wherever, a town, a city, a farm, a church,

---

[132] That is, a ghost, a spirit.

wherever he went, people laid the sick and hurtin' at his feet, beggin' and pleadin' for new life. Some just wanted to touch his family crest. Others believed that if they got close enough, close enough to be near him, their lives and world would be forever different, renewed and be free!

New Market sure felt different than Newport!

(7:1-23)
Ode to the Old Brown Shack Out Back

Among the crowds were some of the professors and the ELITE. They came from Knoxvul, seekin' Jesus.

They took note that Jesus' people, his hillbillies, were rather different than most other goot folk. Most of the hillbillies wore blue jeans and tee-shirts. Some were people of questionable character. For the most part, they were just plain unknowns. All exhibited the fact that life was hard and not necessarily generous. While most goot folk casually sit down to eat and solemnly say their grace, these hillbillies just jumped in and commenced to eatin', pilin' their plates high with food. *"Hardly ever did any of 'em wash their hands before doing so,"* noted the designated journalist amongst the ELITE.

"Why, look at those hicks!" exclaimed a representative of the ELITE to any one who was within earshot. *"Their fingernails are plumb nasty!"*

One needs to remember that fine and refined

religious folk, like those of the ELITE and the professors, do not approach the dinner table unless their nails are perfectly clean, filed, and polished. To eat otherwise is simply barbaric! They would never dream of buyin' anythin' from the farmers' market because God only knows who has touched food at such places.

The ELITE observed many other traditions - "acts of piety" - or they so-called them.

The wearin' of the flashiest and most expensive clothes on Sunday topped it all. If you dress to the "tee," you need to make sure that your "threads" are seen with only the fit and proper folk. And of course, they, as goot people, would never use an outhouse!

So they axed Jesus, *"Why do you and your people not live accordin' to the Bible where it declares that 'cleanliness is next to godliness'?"*

Jesus gave a light laugh, respondin', *"A mountain woman once prophesied rightly about charlatans and phonies. She foresaw, 'These folks honor their God with their lips, suits, clean fingernails, and their bright and shiny china toilets but their hearts are far from me.' And I'm here to say that in vain they seek to appeal to God, teachin' that their way is the only way, the only truth. Let me tell you the way it is. They've abandoned God's grace and love for the very sake of cleanliness!"*

Jesus continued, now pointin' his blacked lined nailed finger at 'em, *"Ya'll have a fine way of rejectin' the command of God in order to keep your understandin' of truth! Surely ya 'member being learned to cherish and look after your paw and maw? And we all noed that someone who denies their own kin is surely losin' out in the life of love. But no! No! Some of you, while holdin' on to your so-called good reputation by tawlkin' about 'family values,' don't give a rip about other families that are different from you. You tawlk, but nothin' happens. You tawlk, but that's all we get. So how in the world can you tawlk about cleanliness and godliness when your own tradition is full of dirty hate and ungodly love? Now don't get me started!"*

Jesus turned the direction of his words to the crowd that had gathered around, *"Listen to me, all of ya'll. Try to understand that there is nothin' outside a person that by goin' in can belittle and degrade. Dirty fingernails or blue jeans ain't goin' to make anybody dirty. What will make a person dirty is what comes out of their mouth, out of their hearts, and how they act with others. What comes out will just about tell you everythin' you need to know about 'em!"*

Jesus finished his speech and left the crowd, findin' a shade on the front screened-in porch of Sister Hicks, a local hillbilly. Here some people gathered around and axed Jesus about what he said.

In reply, Jesus offered, *"Do you not know your decipherin' and your geszintas?*[133] *Do you not understand that whatever geszinta a person from outside cannot make 'em*

---

[133] Deciphering is Southern for doing arithmetic. Geszintas is the mathematical process of division, "Two geszinta four two times," etc.

bad. The reason is that things from the outside don't enter the heart, but the stomach. And what gesz̧inta the stomach goes out into the outhouse. You don't need Sears and Roebuck to have that delivered, now do ya? It is what comes out of the person's heart that is the true picture of their life and their understandin' of love. For it is from within, from the human heart, that evil intentions come - like abuse, theft, murder, unfaithfulness, greed, dishonesty, fraud, lust, rape, resentment, bigotry, arrogance, and lack of love. When these come out, you better watch out and not step in it! And yes, remember to pinch your nose!

All these evil things come from within. They tell the Kodak moment of a person's heart. Dirty fingernails, blue jeans and flannel shirts don't make a person. Don't ever forget that!"

(7:24-30)
A Yankee Visits Jesus

From there, Jesus set out for Maynerdvul.[134]

He arrived and entered the home of Maggie and George.

Jesus tried to keep his visit a secret. He didn't want to make trouble for Maggie an'em. By now, Jesus was considered a rabble-rouser, a troublemaker, a false prophet, and yes, a commie! But despite his best efforts, he couldn't escape notice.

A woman, of Northern raisin' and a "draw"

---

[134] Maynardville, Tennessee.

to go with it, had a daughter with AIDS. She heard that Jesus was at her neighbors' house. She came and fell at Jesus' feet, pleadin' for God to hope.

She and her daughter were financially strapped because of the related medical costs. By now the daughter was dyin', near death.

Jesus was moved with compassion and axed, *"Do you think that God cares about Yankees?"* He asked this not out of contempt, but out of love. Jesus knew that it had been hard for southerners to appreciate their northerner sisters and brothers.

"Yes!" she replied, *"Granted, we are all bastards, but God loves us anyway.*[135] *I've been wondering, though. It just might be that we think we are bastards, but God knows different. Either way, it means that God loves us whether we eat Boston baked beans or fried chicken!"*

Jesus smiled and nodded in approval, *"My dear sister, you believe and understand the mystery of God's love and freedom much more than most. No question about it! We'll find care for your daughter!"*

The woman returned home with hope.

There she took her dyin' daughter into her arms, cryin' and tellin' her daughter about the encounter of Jesus and God's goot news. Her daughter then cried as well. They had been "sick and tired" way too long.

The mother's tears once shed out of

---

[135] Will Campbell, *Brother to a Dragonfly* (New York: Continuum Publishing Group, Inc., 1977), 220.

resignation and pain, now flowed out of a renewed sense of hope, for a pain-stricken daughter and a grieving parent.

Being "sick and tired of bein' sick and tired" pushes one too close to takin' your own life like Katie did. Years ago, a young woman by the name of Kate couldn't handle life any more. Takin' one's own life in these mountains happened far too often than kin wanted to admit.

This mother and daughter, though, had found new life in God's freedom. It's a shame that Katie's pain muffled the sound of God calling her name.

(7:31-37)
The Cost of Freedom

From there, Jesus made his way to "Lizzy Town," in Upper East Tennessee. In Elizabethton, word reached the people about Jesus and his proclamation of God's kingdom--God's hope, freedom, and goot news! And about God's hillbillies!

It was there that a woman, who had been physically and sexually abused for years, was brought to Jesus by some carin' friends.

At first, at the hand of her father, and now her husband of twelve years, abuse was the norm, not the exception. She no longer had 20/20 ears to hear that freedom was her promise from God, free simply to be.

Just be.
Nothing else.
Nothing more.
Just be free.

If it can't be heard and spoken, it can't be experienced. And if it can't be experienced, it can't be spoken!

Up and until now, she felt like her feet had been nailed to the floor.[136]

Jesus took her aside.

Alone, just the two of them.

Jesus respected her person and didn't want to "hang family laundry in public." Their conversation was about God's freein' notion and a new family of acceptance within God's kingdom.

With hands lifted upward, Jesus looked towards the heavens. It was at this moment that she heard the words of her goot news from God. For the first time, she saw an opportunity for a new life and she spoke aloud that freedom! For the first time, she heard her name called from the heavens above!

(I can't explain it! I'm only reporting it!)

Then Jesus ordered everyone to be careful of how they share the goot news. He reminded 'em that others are not as enthused with the people bein' new creatures.

---

[136] See Janesse Ray, *Ecology of a Cracker Childhood* (Minneapolis: Mildweed Editions, 1999), 128.

"*Beware!*" he demanded. "*Some understand, others don't.*"

There was one thing for sure, though. Everyone was astonished by how easy the kingdom of God was a reality among 'em. They now heard words that were once so faint. Now many spoke and lived with courage and gall.

(8:1-13)
Dinner on the Ground

Again, there were more people gatherin' around Jesus than you could shake a stick. Though each heart and soul had been fed with the nourishment of God's goot news, their stomachs growled from a lack of vittles.

Jesus called for the hillbillies and placed a seed in their hearts and ears by sayin': "*Now I am really beginnin' to feel for these folks. They been with us for three days prayin', inquirin', and the like, but their bellies, and mine too, are making more racket than a John Deere diesel tractor. No one can think and pray rightly on an empty belly. For sure, it's hard to hear over all the growlin'.*

So hear me out.

If we send them away right now, some will find themselves too weak for the journey. For if'n you can't think on and over an empty growlin' belly, you sure can't walk with one."

"*But how do you feed when you ain't got some vittles?*" they were askin' amongst 'demselves.

The consensus among the hillbillies was that since you can't get blood from a turnip, you can't get vittles when the cupboard is bare to the bone.

One of 'em reminded Jesus, *"There ain't enough bread in our pockets to satisfy a cheese-filled rat. And besides, Jesus, do you see a Waffle House any where around?"*

Realizin' that the seed wasn't takin' root, Jesus replied, *"I don't care much for turnips. I like my hash browns covered and smothered. I wonder, though, how much bread do we exactly have?"*

"Seven loaves," came the answer amongst the small gatherin'.

So Jesus instructed everyone to find a place on the ground and get comfortable, ready and set. Set and ready to eat.[137]

Jesus took the seven loaves of *Flowers* bread and offered thanks for both the hands that had prepared and earned 'em. He opened the packages and axed his hillbillies to distribute 'em amongst the crowd.

In the meantime, someone found some fish that no one knew was around.

Jesus thanked God for the fish.

And the fish, too, was given out.

Again it happened.

Everyone ate and was filled to the brim. Maybe the fish was bream!

---

[137] This must be where churches first got the idea of dinner on the ground.

It was a rather simple miracle!

There was a whole lot of thanksgivin' and eatin' goin' on.

There had to be at least four thousand people gathered there.

Jesus sent all of 'em away with minds, hearts, and bellies--full!

Followin' this, Jesus and his hillbillies made their way eastward towards Sevier County. There the ELITE came and started an argument with Jesus about the *"price of eggs in China."* They already noed because they had been "Peking" at the prices.

Well, that is not exactly how they started the argument, but they just as well. They wanted Jesus to expound upon his authority and present a sign from the heavens that would legitimize his teachin's about freedom and his proclamation of goot news. But like folks in other places, the folk in Sevier County were more concerned about their lives and the lives of their children - not the price of eggs in China. It's kind of funny that way. What seems so slap-dab excitin' to a few is no more than expelled gas for most.

Jesus didn't want to make light of his inquisitors in front of God and everybody, even though he was tempted. He shook his head in disgust and muttered, *"Why? Why are so many concerned about things that wont' begin to touch people and change their lives, while ignorin' the things that do and can? A sign?*

Why they wouldn't know a sign if one came and introduced itself. If they don't noed the difference between a loaf of bread and a Rhode Island Red, how are they gonna know a sign? A sign? Indeed!"

So Jesus walked off, leavin' them to their egg countin'.

(8:14-26)
A Discourse on Bread, Chickens, and Everythang Else

As Jesus and his hillbillies walked to their next destination, and as the journey lingered, food, again, became a concern.

They had only a single loaf of *Flowers* bread and no Rhode Island Reds!

Jesus observed and commented: *"Bread! Bread! Everyone needs bread. Keep your eyes open for the 'bread' of the ELITE and the Governor."*

"What in the world is he talkin' about?" they axed amongst themselves. *"It's not our fault that we ain't got no bread!"* came a plea from amongst the group. It could be that they thought that Jesus was fussin' about the fact that they had only one loaf of bread.

Jesus said to 'em, *"Why in Sam Hill's name are you tawlkin' about having no bread? I guess you just don't get it, do you? Do your eyes keep you from seein'? Those floppy things on the side of your head, do they keep you from hearin'? Is your memory as long as one of Elizabeth Taylor marriages?*

Think about this!

When we gave the five loaves to the five thousand people, how many cardboard boxes were left?"

They innocently replied, *"Twelve?!"*

"And the seven loaves for the four thousand people, how many bushel baskets were left?"

As their answer came, you could see the chicken feather in the fox's mouth. Slowly gettin' the point, they responded, *"Seven!"*

"I hope you do understand now!" Jesus answered. *"Now get that fedder out of your mouth."*

They went to Dandridge.

A blind man was led to Jesus. The man pleaded for Jesus to help. Jesus took the blind man by the hand and led him out of the company of everyone.

He touched the man's eyes with a mixture of spit and red clay dirt, axin', *"Can you see now?"*

"Yep! I sure do!" he exclaimed but added, *"I see 'em. But they look more like Rhode Island Reds than people."*

Jesus touched his eyes again, with more spit and more dirt. His sight was completely restored. The man could now see the difference between people and Rhode Island Reds.

"Don't go back into town yet," Jesus done told him.

PREPARIN' GOD'S HILLBILLIES
(8:27-38)
Billy Graham, Oral Roberts, Benny Hinn,
*   Home Grown Maters and Rhode Island Reds*

Jesus and his hillbillies continued on the journey, heading towards the Tri-Cities area. As they strolled along a mountain road, Jesus axed a rather innocent question: *"What are people sayin' about me? What names are they callin' me?"*

Each had a different answer.

"Some think that you're as good a pracher as Billy Graham."

"I heard someone axed if you are ordained by the church. They said that you just don't look and act like a regular pracher because you don't wear a tie," said another.

"Someone ask me, 'Who does he think he is, Oral Roberts?'"

"I heard somethin' that will top that. My neighbor thinks that you are another Benny Hinn!"

So Jesus turned the question towards 'em, *"Who do you think and say that I am?"*

Shorty quickly answered, *"You be the one to git us all out of this here mess!"*

Jesus again told 'em to be careful of how they spoke. He began to reveal to 'em that he will undergo tremendous sufferin' and be slighted by the church leaders and other cronies. They will try to kill the message of freedom either by public ridicule or claim that the message is nothin' more than "taters without gravy" or a "bore hog with teats."

"*Though it may at first appear dead, the message of God's hope, freedom, and goot news will become more alive than ever. It and I will live in your hearts and lives, and in your chilren's hearts and lives and even your chilren's chilren,*" he said.

He spoke openly and honestly about all this.

Shorty, however, was upset with the seemin' pessimism of Jesus.

He took Jesus aside and scolded him for such negative thoughts. "*Besides,*" Shorty insisted, "*Norman,*" (another would-be and popular pracher) "*will not continue to follow such gloomy and pessimistic thinkin'.*"

Turnin' away and now addressin' all the hillbillies, Jesus responded to Shorty, "*You've left your plow out in the rain too long and now it's rusted. You are more concerned with what people are a thinkin' than you are interested in lovin' other folk.*"

Jesus then started to sang.

Others crowded around Jesus and the hillbillies because of the commotion.

When Jesus finished sangin', "*No One Likes Eating at a Sad Cafe,*" he added. "*If anyone wants to become one of my hillbillies, let 'em deny their pursuit of wealth, fame, glory, and take up their hurtin's, and follow me in standin' beside and livin' with their brother and sister of the mountains.*

For those who want to save their life by pretendin' that money can buy love and homegrown maters will miss out on both. But those who live lives of love, gratitude and freedom, and who appreciate the small but precious pleasures like home grown maters, will find life. For those who stand with their brother and sister of the hills, who become my hillbillies, those who believe in God's hope and freedom, God will redeem 'em, sanctify 'em, and call 'em by their own names!

For what does it profit a person to hoard all the homegrown 'maters but never eat 'em? For what goot is it to bake a fresh blackberry cobbler and have no one to share it? And what goot is it to have iced tea without ice? What does a person gain by ignorin' the mercy of God and the freedom of brother and sister?

Don't listen to the Style Section of the Knoxvul News Sentinel!

Listen to the loneliness of your soul!

What can be more valuable than life truly lived in freedom? Tell me and tell me now! What can you offer more than your love and your life? I don't need your money. I don't want your fancy designer clothes! I won't accept your credit cards! Anythin' but your love and life is just not acceptable! And why? 'Cause your brothers and sisters of the hills need you, and more importantly, you need 'em. Only then will you save your life, if it's yours to save!"

Jesus wound down, "Shame on you who have changed my words into nice little things that nice little people recite on nice little Sundays! Don't pollute my words with self-interest and greed. For if you do, 'shamie, shamie on you!' For you will probably never see God's freedom in your midst. Your selfishness and greed will prevent you from *knowin' the difference between a loaf of bread and a Rhode Island Red!"*

(9:1-13)
Jesus, Johns, Parks and Jordan - What a Team!
Just when you think Jesus was finished.
"And ain't that a fact! Most of ya'll standin' here will get to know God's hope and freein' power long before McCarty's Mortuary knows ya!"
For sure, he was finished singin' now.
Almost a week later, six days to be exact, Jesus took Jimmie Lee, Shorty, and EvelynAnn up to Clingman's Dome in the Smoky Mountains.
Here they witnessed somethin' that they have never seen. Before their six eyes, Jesus' appearance changed. His clothes dazzled and glistened in the mixture of the shiny misty fog and golden morning sunlight.
Standin' before their wide open eyes, appeared three other people, talkin' to Jesus, Vernon Johns,[138] Rosa Parks,[139] and the other was Clarence Jordan.[140]
Now Jimmie Lee was simply overwhelmed by

---

[138] The predecessor of Dr. Martin Luther King, Jr. at Dexter Avenue Baptist Church in Montgomery, Alabama, Rev. Johns is considered to be the father of the civil rights movement.

[139] Rosa Park's refusal to give up her seat to a white on December 1, 1995 propelled the 381-day Montgomery bus boycott. As a result of the boycott, the Supreme Court ruled segregation on transportation, unconstitutional.

[140] Along with his wife, Florence and Martin and Mabel England, Jordan founded Koinonia Farm in Americus, Georgia based upon equality of races, pacifism, and common resources. Jordan is also author of the Cotton Patch Gospels.

the experience, sight, and sounds. He said to Jesus, *"Jesus! Good God!! I mean, it's wonderful that this has happened! Now what we*
need to do is to make this a holy place. We can build a retreat center up here and let every one have the same experience that we have just had!"

Jimmie Lee was always thinkin' about ways to promote Jesus' message. Jimmie Lee always tawlked before thinkin', too. The other two remained speechless with their jaws restin' on the ground down around their feet!

The fog rolled in thicker and thicker.

The morning sun was quickly lost behind the thick fog and misty clouds. Then, seemingly out from behind the fog and mist, Jimmie Lee, Shorty, and EvelynAnn heard a voice say, *"This is my boy! You can call him Junior if you like. But most of all, give ear to him!"*

Just as quickly as the fog rolled in and the voice bellowed, Johns, Parks, and Jordan disappeared into the mist that was gone!

Now only the original four visitors to the mountain remained.

As they came down from the mountains into Gatlinburg, Jesus insisted that the three not say a word about the mountain top experience, *"Think about it but if you tawlk about it now, most will not understand and will simply accuse you of being crazy. Mum's the word!"*

105

So they did, that is, they kept their mouths shut.

But all the while, they pondered about what happened to Jesus and to 'em. Then they axed Jesus, *"Why do the professors say good and nice things about Vernon Johns, Rosa Parks, and Clarence Jordan all the while swappin' howdies with SAM. The very SAM that both you and 'em warned us about?"*

Jesus answered, *"Well, I'm not sure. You'll have to ask 'em for yourselves. I guess, though, God's freein' notion is threatenin' to both politicians and religious leaders alike. The thought of losin' power, prestige, and influence for the sake of God's freein' notion will surely cause a stink. Johns and Jordan were a couple of the first prophets proclaimin' God's freedom for God's hillbillies - black, white, and red. They each hoped for the restoration of dignity and respect for all peoples. Parks, on the other hand, was tired of all the bad stuff and decided to sit on it!*

But look at things now!

God's freedom is still being thumped and trifled. But I tell you that even in the announcements of love and freedom spoken by 'em, some people spit with indifference and shrug their shoulders."

(9:14-30)
A Young Boy at Ripley's

The four walked over to rejoin the other hillbillies at the *Ripley's Believe It or Not* in downtown Gatlinburg.

Right there at the entrance, a commotion broke out.

A huge crowd of inquirin' on-lookers quickly gathered.

However, as Jesus approached, the crowd forgot about the commotion and turned to greet him. Jesus axed, *"What's the buzz? Sounds like I just walked into a hornet's nest and all the hornets have all the say-so!"*

Someone from the crowd emerged, franticly saying *"Hey, Junior! Jimmie Lee told me that it is all right to call you that. Anyway, well, Jesus, my boy needs doctorin' but I ain't got any money. Sometimes he just ain't right. Sometimes he can't tawlk and other times he just loses all control of his body. He falls to the ground, den his eyes roll up into his head and he nearly bites off his tongue. He just lies there without movin', like he be dead! I axed some of your hillbillies if they could help, but they couldn't."*

Jesus was moved and said, *"Why is it that many of God's hillbillies are deprived of the simplest of care? Bring me the boy."*

The boy was brought to him.

Then the boy fell to the ground with his eyes rollin' up into his head, exposin' only the whites of his eyes.

The child was motionless.

Jesus stooped down upon his knees to cradle the boy in his arms, and axed, *"How long has this been goin' on?"*

"*Almost from day one,*" came a weak reply from the father and he continued. "*We really have to keep an eagle eye on the boy. Sometimes he might hurt himself. Other times we don't know if he will come back to us. Can you hope us? I mean, can you hope the boy?*"

"*With God's goot news, just about all things are possible and probable.*"

And then the boy's father cried out, "*O Jesus, I really trust in God. I really do, but sometimes trustin' just won't pay the rent.*"

The crowd was now really pressin' in and all around, hopin' to get a glimpse of the action.

Jesus, then, did something that surprised everyone around the sit'ation.

Still cradlin' the boy, Jesus brought him closer to his bosom and whispered softly in his ear. To this day, no one knows for sure what Jesus said.

Jesus laid the boy back down on the pavement. He took him by the hand and gently lifted him to his feet.

The boy stood and began to tawlk with his father.

The boy was made whole.

Jesus then quickly departed from the crowd with his hillbillies a few steps behind, followin'.

Some axed amongst 'emselves why they couldn't do what Jesus just done. Stoppin' and turnin,' Jesus said, "*First things first!*"

That's all he said.

They walked from Gatlinburg and passed through Cocke County.

Regardin' the healin' of the boy, all Jesus would say was, *"I don't care to tawlk about hit right now."*

(9:31-50)
Watch Out for Hornets' Nests
"Be on the look out!" Jesus said, *"You had better watch for hornets and their nests. There are some who are as mad as hornets, because of what we are sayin' and what God is a'doin.'"*

Things were startin' to git a little rough for Jesus by now.

Jesus began to expect the worst, so he confessed, *"I'm sure that they are plottin' somethin'. They are up to somethin'. They will kill me either by force or by word of mouth. Either way, they'll think that will be the end of me and the message of God's freedom and goot news for the hillbilly. But don't you dare put an ounce of stock into it. Don't you ever believe it. Though they kill me, God's freein' notion will live on in some form or fashion. So you watch out!"*

Some didn't understand. Some understood all too well.

Either way, you have to admit it's too hard to think about such a thang and even harder to tawlk about it. Dyin' ain't a favorite subject amongst any one.

And for most, other pressing things are on

their minds.
Like...

Jesus and his hillbillies returned to Dandridge. There they rested.

Evidently some had been talkin' quite passionately and loudly behind Jesus' back. Jesus was curious, so he axed, *"What's all this chewin' about? Are you discussin' the difference between a loaf of bread and a Rhode Island Red again? Put your cookies on the table. Don't hide them! Hit don't do no goot to hide 'em!"*

No one really wanted to do that. They were embarrassed for Jesus overheard what they was a'sayin'. For during the journey back to Dandridge, their discussin', cussin', and fussin' was about which one of 'em was the "bestest"[141] hillbilly.

"Say what?" Jesus axed with disgust. *"Who's the best hillbilly, you say? Well, why didn't you just axe in the first place? Follow me. I don't want all that good discussin,' cussin' and fussin' to be all in vain."*

They all went out of the house out into the yard where some children were playin' kick the can. Jesus sat down in the middle of the yard amongst the kids.

"Now," Jesus began to explain. *"Be careful out here because I believe that I've seen a hornet or two buzzin' around ya'll's heads. Remember, first things first. And puttin' first things first means...."*

---

[141] Akin to "the goodest of the bunch," but much better.

Jesus, however, was interrupted with a child jumpin' unexpectedly on to his lap.

The child smiled with her white teeth a'shinin' in deep contrast to her dark skin. Jesus returned the smile and embraced her.

Jesus continued, *"First things first, just like I told and just like this here child has done. First things first. Be that way and you will welcome every child and everyone else. Everyone! For if you reject the child, you reject your brother and sister. You also reject me as well as the one who sends me! Be free!"*

Shorty said to Jesus, *"Junior!"*

Shorty loved callin' Jesus that because he feels like he is gettin' away with somethin'. *"We came across some folks the other day speakin' about God's freedom and goot news, sayin' some of the same things that you are sayin'. But that bunch tawlked funny. They say that there ain't no hell! Hell-far!* [142] *They say that they be "ho-hellers,"* [143] *but I don't reckon I take a God that don't get pissed every now and then! We tried to stop 'em because we hadn't approved of 'em. You know, you have to be careful who you let in."*

Jesus halfway smiled and replied, "Shortshanks!"

Jesus loved calling him by that name because he knew Shorty loathed it.

---

[142] Fire.

[143] Primitive Baptists of Central Appalachia that does not believe in hell beyond the grave, see Howard Dorgan, *In The Hands of a Happy God* (Knoxville: University of Tennessee, Knoxville, 1997).

"*Watch out! I believe I just heard the buzz of a couple more hornets. Now as to those strangers, no need to stop 'em, because they are our kin. Though they tawlk funny, they are spreadin' the goot news that we are spreadin'. Besides, it is kind of hard to say bad about a person while embracin' 'em. So don't forget, that whoever is willin' to embrace God's freein' way can't be a'gin us! And don't be so jealous! Remember that jealous man back in the olden days. He was so jealous of Eldad and Medad,[144] that his face turned green.*

You probably don't remember that story but at least check it out.

It might teach you somethin.'

Just because someone don't wear a flannel shirt don't mean that they are not your kin. And just the same, not everyone who is not a'gin you is necessarily a hillbilly.

Watch out for those hornets and their nests!

And don't play with water moccasins and matches! And while I'm a tawlkin', if our jealousy stands to block or trip God's freedom, shame on you! Blockin' and trippin' is plain foolishness and dangerous. So, my brothers and sisters remember, it's best to be thought a hillbilly than to speak foolishly and remove all doubt. Hits better to go through life bein' thought to be a hillbilly than allowin' your hands, feet and eyes to do foolish things and remove all wonder.

And this P.S.!

Don't forget about your mouth and tongue. They have the greater tendency in revealin' one's true foolishness.

---

[144] See Numbers 11:27.

Such foolishness of jealousy is both the home to water moccasins and bonfars. If you get too close, both will take bite of you!

We are not in a foot race here! You're already at the finish line. All that is left for us is to celebrate.

Celebrate the freedom God is agivin' ya! Celebrate God's a'doin's!

Celebrate your brother and sister's freedom, too! Then you will be at peace with one another! Remember that nobody can take either of 'em away from ya! I'm finished singin' now!"

(10:1-16)
Why Are You Worried About Burnt Biscuits

Jesus left and went to the northern area of Sevier County, just east of Douglas Lake.

As to his whereabouts, news traveled like a runaway far.

Jesus was greeted once again with a throng of people. Unable to deny his southern hospitality and upbringin', he welcomed each and every one and told them of God's freedom and goot news.

Some of the ELITE caught wind of his arrival.

They axed him, *"Is it lawful for a man to divorce his wife?"*

"Well," Jesus responded, *"What did the people of old say?"*

"That's easy," came a reply, *"If a wife burns the*

biscuits, then that's enough grounds to get shed of her."

There was a loud outburst of laughter with enough back and knee slappin' to accompany all the chucklin' of the ELITE.

An unsolicited response arose amongst the laughter, *"Just tell the judge and he'll understand!"* There was more knee slappin'.

"I guess you be right," Jesus replied.

"I guess, though, that since marriage is only for the sake of convenience and sex, then you will continue to treat women only as means for your own gain.

But that's not what God had in mind.

Marriage is to be surrounded with care, compassion, understandin', and commitment. Don't sound like much commitment when you are more interested in burnt biscuits. Anytime that you are more interested in burnt biscuits than about the life of people, you ain't on the straight and narrow!"

Later on, some of the hillbillies axed Jesus about this conversation.

"You see," Jesus, answered tenderly, *"marriage needs to be one of commitment, not hurtin'. God is mighty upset with goin'ons that hurt folks."*

People then brought their little ones to Jesus in order that he might touch and bless them. Some tried to stop the intrusion. Jesus got angry when he saw what was a happenin' and snapped, *"Let these little children come! Don't you know that the kingdom belongs to such? Don't you know that the kingdom belongs*

to those who the world would rather silence and ignore? *Don't you know that the kingdom belongs to those that are a'hurtin'? Unless you become like one of these - no, better yet - unless you become a hillbilly, you will never see or enter the kingdom!"*
    With that, Jesus hugged the gatherin' children.

(10:17-27)
You Can't Hold a Baby With Your Arms Full
    As Jesus was preparin' to set out for Knoxvul, a quite wealthy young man came up and fell before him, and axed, *"Good Teacher, I want to be a hillbilly. I want to know of a better life. I know that money can't buy love and homegrown 'maters! So tell me what I need to do to be one of your hillbillies."*
    Oddly and strangely enough though, this young man had a habit of carryin' all of his wealth and thangs in a cardboard box tucked under his arms.
    Everything.
    All of it.
    He never did trust anyone with what he worked so hard to get.
    As he knelt, he clutched the worn, tattered and crumpled Moon-Pie cardboard box under his right arm.
    "Well, well, I don't know whether I am that goot," exclaimed Jesus. *"God is definitely goot, so let's holt out on this 'goot teacher' stuff. Anyway, so you are lookin' fer*

somethin' different?
Let's see how bad.
Do you know the commandments? 'Nary kill a person; respect the mystery of sex; don't be a thief and a cheat; don't speak bad of kinfolk and neighbors; don't say one thing and do another; be goot to your momma and daddy?"

"Absolutely, Jesus. I not only know 'em, I follow 'em. I have tried to follow 'em since I was knee-high to a grasshopper. I learnt about 'em in Sunday School. I really liked Sunday School," he cheerfully and proudly responded.

Of course, he was stretching the truth a bit. Sex is never discussed in Sunday school!

Jesus looked deep into the man's eyes and stared straight into the heart of his soul.

Jesus felt like the boy's daddy and said, "Well, that's great and don't that beat all! You're almost a hillbilly. I'll tell you what. The only other thing left to do is to go over there and pick up little Rori, Bill and Crystal's little baby girl.[145] That's all you have to do."

"That's all?"

"That's all!"

The young man raced over to Rori but could do nothin'.

Holdin' Rori meant droppin' his box.

---

[145] Rori is probably one of the "preddiest" little girls you ever laid eyes on. The difference between "pretty" and "preddy" is mighty big. You could use "pretty" to describe spring flowers, but spring flowers don't even compare to "preddy" little Rori.

The box, however, was too valuable to him. It was too important.

Jesus stood with the onlookers and whispered in the ear of one standin' by, *"Do you think that he believes when he dies that he will put his money in traveler's checks?"*

Jesus hurt inside hisself for the man, though. The young man disappeared into the throng of people, unable to hold little Rori and unable to become a hillbilly.

Those gathered were stunned and troubled by the turn of events.

So Jesus, sensin' their distress, said, *"My brothers and sisters, my kin, God's freein' notion is both easy and difficult. Sometimes it is as easy as holdin' a little baby. But it's awfully hard to hold a baby with your arms full. Besides, it might be easier for a mule to pass through an eyedropper than it is for a person with full arms to become a hillbilly."*

"Then, who can be a hillbilly?" came a question from the crowd.

"The beginnin' of God's freein' notion is a like square dance. By definition, you can't have a dance without company. That goes for you and God. It takes you to respond to God's freein' power in order for a dance to break out. Are you ready to dance? I hear the fiddle strings warmin' up!"

(10:28-31)
I Ain't Got a Dime Now

    Shorty then said, *"Now, Jesus, we have left everythin' to follow you. Since I met you, I ain't got a dime to my name."*

    Jesus noed this and said, *"Money is hard to come by when you give priority to God's freedom. But let me remind you that I didn't promise one dime or a gazillion dimes. I don't make those kind of promises. What I did promise is the notion of life beyond measure, even beyond the measure of a stinkin' dime. Remember that God is a'turnin' this world upside down. What is first now, will be last later. When the dime is turned over, then you will see that which is now last will be first!"*

    That's what Jesus said.

(10:32-45)
Those Pesky Hornets

    As they continued towards Knoxvul, Jesus walked a few strides ahead of those in tow.

    He liked to walk fast.

    Now those who had become hillbillies were beginnin' to get a little shaky about all this death business. Well, they were really awe-struck about the freedom and transformation that they was experiencin', but you know that can be a frightenin' thing, too.

    Sensin' that some of the hillbillies were a'swattin' at flies that had not yet lit, Jesus came to a complete stop, and then said, *"Now, lookie here, just as a maple leaf turns up to receive a comin' rain, know for sure that there are some hornets up ahead. They don't like what I've been sayin' and doin' and not sayin' and not doin'.*

Don't be surprised if they handcuff me and haul my ole rusty hide over to the jailhouse. Mark my words, they are goin' to try to make me out to be the laughin'stock of Tennessee. Well, not THE laughin'stock--there's already too much snickerin' going on in Nashvul.

Anyway, they're goin' to make it look like my mama done went and raised a fool!

Don't be shocked at what they will say about me or do to me. You might be careful because your hobnobbin' with me is goin' to get you treated the same way.

Don't worry!
Don't fret!
God will lift up what they bury!
There is a rain a comin'! Look at the leaves!
And in the midst of that rain, there are some angry hornets!"

Evidently, Johnny and Jimmy, sons of Zeb, must have been preoccupied with more important things. One axed Jesus, *"Now, Jesus, we've been thinkin', we think that we have been quite loyal to you. So now, when you come into your power, will you do for us what we have done for you?"*

"Now," replied Jesus. *"I know what you have done. What is it that you want me to do for you two?"*

"Well," responded the other. *"How about makin' one of us your chief secretary and the other in charge of your security when you rise to the top!"*

"Are you sure?" Jesus inquired. *"Are you sure that you can sip from the same gourd that I'm sippin'? Are you sure that you can stand the same rain water that's about to come my way?"*

In unison, they shouted, *"You're dang straight we can!"*

"Then, I guess you will be sippin' from the same gourd and will be covered with the same rain! But I reckon that the other formal stuff will be left to those who are prepared for it!"

Now the other hillbillies got wind of that conversation and thought it was quite bold, if not, snotty of Jimmy and Johnny to axe for such things.

Jesus interjected and added, *"Now lookie here! You know for the most part, in our lives there have been plenty of people who have decided and tried to fashion who we are and who we are goin' to be! There's plenty of bosses, foremen, supervisors, bureaucrats, and other people who have nothin' more to do than run your life for you.*

You know that's right!

Remember, however, you are different! You are a hillbilly! You're God's hillbilly and with God's hillbillies, if'n you're lookin' to be great, then you're to live like a hillbilly.

Be the trash that will save the world! And know this

to be true, if'n you want to be first, then treat other folks like a hillbilly, God's hillbilly.

I didn't get in this rainstorm for my jollies! I've wanted you to discover your lives, your histories! If it costs me somethin', then so be it. Some may call it a bribe. I call it hope and God's freein' notion!"

(10:46-52)
Ernest and Curious George
The hillbillies made their way through Dandridge and there, a man by the name of Ernest, began to shout at Jesus from the roadside.

"Jesus! God's hillbilly! I need you!"

Many rushed to Ernest and tried to shut him up.

Some thought that you needed to be dignified around Jesus.

You know how some religious leaders can be. They are liable to fight over a coat in an airplane if you don't respect 'em. Don't act like Bobby!

"Be quiet!"
"Be respectful!"
"Shut your dang mouth!" came another demand.

However, Ernest wasn't about to let this opportunity slip by him and shouted even louder, *"Jesus, son of Jed![146] I really need you!"*

Jesus stopped and said, *"I need you, too! Let's*

---

[146] Jed was a famous hillbilly, for those who don't know it.

tawlk."

"He's tawlkin' to you, boy!" came a quick snort amongst the crowd.

Ernest jumped up, throwin' off his plaid, tattered coat to the dirt, and ran to Jesus.

"I know I need you, Ernest," Jesus said. *"But how do you need me?"*

"I'm blinded to letterin' and words, Jesus. I can't read or write. I remember my mama readin' to me about a fella called Curious George. I wish I could read it for myself. But that's been over twenty years ago. I never got to leart how to read. I can't get a job. I can't read the newspaper to find a job. People have taken my money, my possessions, and even my life 'cause I can't read! I beg just to get by!"

"Don't worry about a thing!" Jesus offered in comfort. *"You'll be readin' before you know it! You'll even get to read what Curious George has been doin' for all these years. Your faith in God's freein' notion is about to set you free!"*

"Johnny! Jimmy! Come over here!" instructed Jesus. *"'Member when you wanted somethin' important to do? I've got an important project for the two of you! Help Ernest find George!"*

Ernest joined in as one of God's hillbillies.

FINAL DAYS IN KNOVUL
(11:1-25)
Ramblin' Towards Knoxvul

As they approached Knoxvul, Jesus sent two hillbillies to the H&H Car Mart. He said to 'em, *"Ya'll go there and there ya'll find a hand-painted Rambler wagon. It's black. You can't miss it. Tell Shortarm Sam that I need it. We'll bring it back as soon as we are finished. He'll rightly understand."*

Sure enough, that Rambler was exactly where Jesus said it was to be found. They didn't have any money, but when they said they needed it, Shortarm Sam barked, *"Well, I guess you don't need it as bad as you think you do."*

"Jesus sent us here..."

Before they could finish, Shortarm Sam added, *"Well, why in the dickens didn't you say so in the first place? Here's the keys. Bring it back when you are finished. And here's a ten spot for a full tank of gas."*

They took that hand-painted Rambler back to the rest of the folks and Jesus. You would have thought that it was a limousine the way everyone carried on about it.

Jesus jumped on the hood of the car, with Danny, son of a preacher and a hillbilly's grandson, driving it. Ammie was helping with directions.

The people followed behind it.

Singin'.

Clappin'.

Dancin' God's goot news as they made their

way to Knoxvul.

Even Preston, Spencer, Tyler, and Ammie's Justin - all Danny's youngin's, joined in the parade of dancers.

Occasional rounds of *"Rocky Top"* broke out in waves of spontaneous pandemonium. For the moment, all was right with the world.

They stopped at a nearby church for prayers and rest. Now quite late, they made their way over to Sevier Heights, the outskirts of Knoxvul.

The next day they entered the First Church of High Society in downtown Knoxvul.

Jesus created a stir.

Some called it an act of ecclesiastical disobedience.

Some called it verbal vandalism.

Some others simply called it *"hell-raisin'!"*

Others saw it as an act of prayer.

Others were just stunned.

Jesus accused the church leadership and its congregation of racial and class snobbery.

He said, *"You have swapped God's goot news for a pinkie extension as you sip your afternoon tea! You think that you are God's people because you call upon God. I'm here to tell and show you that God's people are not racist, bigoted, nor nose-raisers! The kingdom of God is a place for all people, whether they smell pretty or stink, whether they have shoes or not! By the name of the livin' and lovin' God, this place will never again blossom in this world. God's goot news is here to stay!"*

You talk about ruffled feathers.

At this point the ELITE decided that 'nuff is 'nuff.

"You can't have a lunatic goin' around and makin' a mockery out of the church," they said. *"Nor can you have this lunatic fillin' people with such foolish notions!"*

Later Jesus spied a dogwood tree.

Jesus said to it, *"Why don't you have your white blossoms? It would be nice to see such beauty this time of the year."*

Those who overheard Jesus talkin' thought that the *"cheese was about to slide off Jesus' cracker."* It was not time for the blossoms.

"Never again," Jesus barked to the tree, *"never again will you have blossoms."*

"His cheese has slid off his cracker," muttered a by-stander. *"He's done gone tawlkin' to dogwoods!"*

They rested that night.

The next mornin', they saw the dogwood tree had withered away to its roots.

Shorty remembered what Jesus said, *"Jesus, ain't that a sight for sore eyes! That dad-gone dogwood tree is withered up like a politician's career. You said it would."*

Jesus then replied, *"God's power is real. It ain't just a notion of my mind, nor of yours. It is a matter of the heart. God can even take a heart like Shortarm Sam's and make a difference with him. Some had said that would have been easier to command the Smoky Mountains to jump into the Atlantic Ocean than for Sam to change. It's real! Believe me! But Shorty, pay less attention to that dogwood!"*

(11:26-33)
Don't Ever Say Somethin' Bad about Family

They was "greeted" by a large gatherin' of some of the folks of the seminar.

A spokesperson for 'em inquired of Jesus, *"By whose name are you stirrin' up things? Who made you God? Who gave you the right to make such accusations?"*

"Now," Jesus offered in return, *"you're askin' some mighty important questions. If you will answer my question, then I will be tickled pink to answer your question."*

"Alright 'den."

"Was John Bob of God or just a lunatic?"

The spokesperson huddled with his group for a reply.

"Now if we say that John Bob was of God, then Jesus will ask us why we didn't believe him. And if we dare say that John Bob was a lunatic, we might not make it back home because you know how all of these people loved John Bob."

After huddlin', the spokesperson turned to Jesus and said, *"We just don't know!"*

"Alright 'den." Jesus said and walked away.

(12:1-12)
Muskedine Wine and other Whines
    Jesus, later, spun a yarn by sayin',
    "Once there was a woman who planted muskedines. Muskedines make good wine, ya noed.
    She didn't just plant to make one glass but wanted to make some money at it as well. She needed some hope in tendin' to the vines, so she got a hopin' hand from her neighbors.
    One day she got word that a relative in Memphis was sick. She left her farm to tend to her sick cousin. Her neighbors said that they would take care of the vines and brin' 'em to harvest if she was gone long enough.
    Hit's hard to beat good neighbors like you,' she said and left in a hurry.
    Her cousin was real sick, so she stayed a spell in Memphis. Knowin' that it was harvest time and such, she sent a friend of her cousin's to get her share of the profit. The messenger from Memphis was greeted neighborly by the neighbors, but when the messenger said that she had come to fetch a share of profit for her friend's cousin, they attacked and beat her.
    She left town within a couple inches of her life and no profit.
    'Are you sure that you went to the right place?' the woman axed the messenger. 'Dem's goot people. Good folk! I'd never dreamed that they would act with such foolishness.'
    So she sent another friend with the address written down on a 5x8 card. Sure 'nuff, the same thing happened, but they even added insult to injury by saying, 'No good comes

from Memphis.'

'My stars and garters, what in the world is goin' on?" she asked herself after hearin' the news from the second messenger.

The woman decided to send her daughter, who now lived in California.

Then Jesus axed those gathered, *"You reckon' that they will hurt her own flesh and blood? If they do, what do you think the woman will do to her neighbors? You know that the mountain woman said that some people are a funny lot. Some people would throw away the very things that they need, even the baby with the bath water."*

The seminar folk didn't cotton too kindly to this story 'cause they took it quite personally. They wanted to show Jesus a thing or two. They were afraid, however, of attackin' and insultin' Jesus. The crowd outnumbered them.

(12:13-37)
Uncle Sam and Other Hounds That Chase

The ELITE sent in reinforcements.

They came to Jesus with a mental trap, hoping to discredit him, publicly.

"Professor," [147] they began, *"We know that your heart is right and that you preach that God's love and freedom is takin' a likin' to all people. Their skin color, their pocket book, and even the way they talk do not mean squat to*

---

[147] Now we both know that they ain't using this term with any sense of endearment.

God....."
    Some one in the crowd was overheard to say, *"Jesus, I like the way you tawwwwwwwlk."*
    Immediately, the crowd erupted into thunderous applause and laughter.
    The trap continued to unfold, *"...Anyway, can you tell us whether we should or should not pay our income taxes? Do you reckon that God wants us to or not?"*
    Jesus knew that the whole thing was stinkin' up to high heaven.
    He inquired, *"Any of you'uns got a five spot?"*
    Someone in the crowd presented a five-dollar bill.
    Jesus asked, *"Whose noggin' do you see on this five spot?"*
    "Lincoln!" came a reply.
    "*Uncle Sam!*" came another.
    "Well, 'den," Jesus said smilin', *"You give Uncle Sam what is his'un 'cause he'll dog it from you anyway. And well with God, give God what's due."*
    The ELITE stood silent.
    Dumbfounded.
    Amazed.
    Speechless.
    Others came with many questions about dead people marryin' and such, about which is the greatest commandment and even about the lineage of King David's kinfolk.
    Jesus responded with a short story:

"We want 'em out and we want them out now!" demanded the unified and united voices.

Once upon a time there was a community of god-fearin' people who wanted all of the hillbillies out of town.

"We want 'em out and we want them out now!"

It was being suggested that the hillbillies took too large a share of the jobs from the good local people. Furthermore, word was spread that these hillbillies were lazy, shiftless and depended on handouts more than anything. No one ever saw the contradiction between the two accusations! Reason means nothing when hate reigns.

The religious leader of the god fearin' folk led the march to the town square demandin' that the officials get rid of these "good-for-nothin'" hillbillies. Being educated, however, the pracher said that things should be done in a dignified and respectful manner. So he proposed a debate--a debate between the town and the hillbillies.

If the hillbillies win the debate, they can stay.

If not, then they had to leave.

The debate, however, would be conducted without words.

Seein' that they had no other options, the hillbillies relented and agreed. They sought out the most intellectual member of their band. No one would step forward because it was a "lose-lose" situation. There was no doubt that the debate was rigged in some way. No one in their right mind would agree to debate and become both the laughin' stock and scapegoat.

Finally, Bubba stepped forward and said, "I ain't got

a thang to lose. We've got everythin' to gain. I'll grab the bull by the horns."

Now Bubba wasn't the brightest star in these heavens, but he was the only one a'willin' to wrastle.

On the day of debate, the town square was filled to capacity. The town square was divided by an imaginary line by the conflictin' loyalties.

The pracher made his way to the center fountain with all the pomp and circumstance due Hulk Hogan. Dressed in his bright, multicolored flowing ecclesiastical robe, his stroll brought shouts and cheers usually reserved for the WWE.[148] The shouts and cheers were ones of confidence. This was a show. And what a show!

Some one in the crowd yelled, "Just as well pass the cryin' towels and the movin' boxes now!" Half of the crowd roared with sarcastic approval.

Bubba's arrival at the center fountain was received with little fanfare. His dress was subdued, at least compared to his foe. His stained, but yet cleaned blue jeans and faded DVD tee shirt paled against the brilliant multicolored rayon robe of his competition.

The circuit judge, appointed by the town council, was the monitor of the debate. She signaled the debate.

It commenced.

The pracher stepped forward.

The crowd roared.

He raised both hands and motioned for silence.

The silence was deafenin.'

---

[148] A.ka., fake wrestling.

He crossed his arms on his chest. With his stature and presence exudin' confidence and power, he raised his right arm towards the heavens and held up three fingers.

The crowd roared, again.

Now it was Bubba's turn.

He stood anxiously and nervously before the throngs of people. He, too, raised his right arm toward the heavens but held up a lone index finger.

Round one was finished.

With the degree-filled robe sleeve flowin' in midsummer breeze, the pracher swept across the horizon with his left arm to begin the second round.

Bubba replied by pointin' to the ground below his mud-clogged brogans.

Round two was finished, too.

With that, the pracher leaped from the stage and ran into his church nearby. Just as quickly as he disappeared into the church, he returned and jumped back onto the make shift stage. Liftin' his left hand to the sky, he revealed the communion chalice. And with his right hand slowly ascendin' as well, he revealed the leftover host.

The crowd erupted in a burst of applause.

The debate had been won without Bubba having to continue, so they thought.

When the noise dissipated, Bubba simply reached into his pocket and revealed a granny smith apple and held it towards the pracher.

In shock and amazement, the preacher exclaimed, "They can stay! Every last one of them can stay! A dang

hillbilly has done gone and made a fool out of me!"
Bubba had won the debate.

And he won the freedom of his people.

Later that evenin', someone approached the disgraced preacher and axed him to interpret the events and actions of the debate.

"Well, when I held up three fingers to say that God is three persons, that dang fool responded with one finger as to say, 'Yes, but the three are one!' Then when I pointed to the sky to suggest that God transcends everythin' that we can say or imagine, Bubba pointed to the ground as if to say, 'Yes, but God is still present with us right where we live.'

Finally, when I presented the wine and bread from Holy Communion to speak of what God has done for us, he presented an apple to remind us that the pride of Adam still lives with us.'"

The pracher just shook his head and added, "Apparently, they pitted me against the shrewdest and cunnin' of them all. Those dern hillbillies would do anything to keep their places."

In turn, back among the hillbilly celebration, Bubba was tellin' his side of the story.

"I'm not sure I completely understood what in the devil was goin' on. But when that fancy dude dressed up like the second comin' held up three fingers as if to say, 'You'uns gots three days to get out of here,' I got scared and said we could be out in one day!'"

And when he swept across the sky as if to say, 'We'll hound your butts from one end of the earth to the next,' I got *mad and said, 'In that case, we'll just stay right here!'"*

When that sucker ran into the church and brought back that food, I showed him my lunch too. Then he said we could stay!" [149]

Someone in the crowd said to Jesus, *"I get it!"*
Jesus replied, *"You are not far from being a hillbilly."*

(12:38-44)
"Give Until You Starve" and Other Misquotes of God
After all this, as they watched the traffic enterin' at the nearby Church of the High Society, Jesus saw an older woman go in, carryin' an offerin' envelope.

This was "money day" at the church.

Jesus called this to the attention of those around him and said, *"Lookie there. Look at all those fancy cars pullin' up at the church.*

Marsades.

BMWs.

Saabs.

You name it.

You noed those people gots to be loaded. And look at that older woman. She ain't got a pot to pee in but she gives as well, even more.

---

[149] We both know that this story is not in the book of Mark, but it does make the point of verses Mark 12:18-37. Story adapted from article entitled "Debate" by Michael Williams in *Biblical Preaching Journal* (Fall 1993), 15-16.

Don't that just bust ya?
Why in the world would the Church of High Society require a woman to give her rent and food money? Everybody else lives high on the hog but because of their greed, they don't mind tellin' this woman that God loves her as she starves and freezes to death.
It ain't no wonder that God gets a bad rap!"

(13:1-37)
Sticks and Stones

When Jesus was near the Church of High Society, one of the hillbillies said, *"Lookie, Jesus! This place is huge! Look at the size of those stones."*

In reply, Jesus said, *"Take a close look at all these here tall buildin's. There's Jake's! C.H's! A.J.'s!* [150] *And even this church! Nary a stone will stand upon another, one of these days; words will be greater than all these stones. Nary a stone will be upon another."*

When they found a restin' spot, EvelynAnn, Shorty, Jimmy and Johnny were completely mesmerized by Jesus' words about the buildin's and axed, *"Tell us! Tell us when all this is goin' to take place. Can you give us a hint? Anythin' that we ought to be lookin' fer?"*

Then Jesus said, *"I noed that we all noed the old sayin', 'Sticks and stones may break my bones but words will*

---

[150] Buildings in Knoxville. A.J. is the old Andrew Johnson Hotel.. Jake and C.H. Butcher were once prominent financiers in Knoxville with their own respective buildings.

never hurt me.'

Well that be mighty right!

Now others will come and try to say that there is a better way for God's freein' notion to come. Don't be misled. There are some who are only interested in what benefits 'em. There will be plenty of times when it seems that the world is goin' to suds in a washtub. There will be fightin', rumors of fightin', wars and rumors of wars. Don't be discouraged! God's love, freedom, and goot news will have the last word. Self-interested leaders and such will slander God's people because they can't stand the notion of change nor the emergence and birth of a God's kingdom on earth. Don't fret, God's ways is greater than anythin' that anyone can chuck and throw away.

God's freedom will be manifested in all the crannies of this world!

Don't be surprised that you might be called all sorts of names! Or better yet, people might call ya redneck-lover, nigger-lover, injin'-lover or queer lover. Even better, they might resort to call you Hillbilly!

You may even find yourself before others, indicted, havin' to defend your stance. Don't worry. God will be with you! God's goot news will give you the courage to be bold and holy.

In the midst of hate, you will find brother pitted against brother, sister estranged from sister, mammas and daddies fighting against children. Hate finds home wherever it can find intolerance and bigotry. You know what being bound up feels and smells like. Be faithful and true, however. The path down God's freedom is not an easy one.

You will hear people proclaimin' the end of the world! We will hear that 'so-and-so' is the incarnation of the anti-Christ. You tawlk about hurlin' stones and tossin' sticks! Don't be alarmed. You know that you have each other and God!

In the midst of it all, recognize the signs.

You don't need a weather rock to detect the signs.

Recognize the signs of hate; for some will try to cloak it in runny, stringy, and tantalizin' sap.

Recognize hurtin'.

We can tell when rain comes by the turnin' up of the leaves, surely we can recognize hurtin' and all its family.

And mind ya, others will come and say that God's kingdom is here or there. Remember that it has already come! You are in its midst. And its midst is in your midst. Let love, understanding and freedom uncover it for you.

Be ready!

Be alert!

Don't let it slip by.

Don't be late.

Hits like the notion of the three wise men. They arrived after the fact. If they had been women, they would have asked for directions and gotten at the manger on time! Remember that timin' is everything."

LYNCHED IN THE JAIL AND CRUCIFIED IN THE PAPERS

(14:1-9)
The Rose of Sharin'

Now it was two days before Thanksgivin'.

The ELITE had been talkin' about and lookin' for ways to get shed of Jesus. Now was not the time, however. There was no reason to bring more attention to this critter, Jesus. At least that was their conclusion.

While in Burlington, visitin' the home of a member of the NAACP, Jesus was approached by a woman carryin' a small vial of homemade perfume. She popped the top and poured just a squeezin' on Jesus' head and began to rub it in his hair.

This offended some of the hillbillies because she seemed to enjoy it just a little too much. Besides, one suggested, she was wastin' somethin' that could be used in a better way. (Perfume made from roses is quite is rather expensive, I can only guess.)

"Why," someone commented, *"we could have sold it and helped our hillbillies in these mountains and in God's kingdom."*

Jesus didn't take too kindly to their outbursts of disdain and jealousy sayin', *"Why in the Sam Hill do you got to trouble this woman? Can't you see that it is the outpourin' of her heart, not the bottle that's going on here? Yes, you could sell it. That's a mighty-fine attitude. But how do you go about showin' your love for one another? Besides, I don't reckon that people will mind a good-smellin' Jesus, do you? She's just sharin' her roses with me while I've still got breath, not when I ain't. I'll bet you two possums on this, that wherever and whenever people come together in the name and power of God's goot news, they will remember this woman."*

Turnin' to the givin' and gracious woman, Jesus added, *"Don't you forget that, Rose."*

(14:10-17)
The Plot and the Gravy Thickens

There was one hillbilly who had more faith in Jesus than anyone else. However, he just felt like that Jesus was movin' too slow in this freein' notion thang. So he conceived of a way where that Jesus would have no other choice but to act, and act now.

With his plot Pat, a.k.a., J.I.--short for Johnny Ichabod, went to speak to the ELITE.

The ELITE was delighted to now have an insider.

Pat was delighted that they thought of him as an insider.

He wasn't.

You wouldn't and couldn't find a man or woman who had more hope, more stock in the power of God that Jesus talked about than him. No, sirree.

No turn coat here in Pat. He was just doin' God's business, or so he thought. He was just buildin' God's club.

Pat noed that Jesus and God would rise to the occasion. Both just needed a little promptin,' a gentle push in the right direction towards SAM.

On the day before Thanksgivin' some hillbillies axed, *"Aren't we goin' to celebrate Thanksgivin'? We need to get ready."*

So Jesus sent two of the hillbillies down on Cumberland Avenue and charged them to say to the first person they met, *"'Is there any place that we could set up a Thanksgivin' party?' And that person will show you a place and there we will make our fixin's."*

Sure enough, it happened just like Jesus said.

Preparations were made.

They were reminded not to forget the gravy for the mashed creamed 'taters.

They didn't.

The gravy was thick, just like Pat liked it.

And the hillbillies gathered that evenin'.

(14:18-26)
"Rocky Top!"

While they were eatin' turkey and dressin' with all the trimmin's, including mashed 'taters, Jesus studied that *"somethin' was up."*

"What do you mean? Is the gravy burnin'?" one axed.

"No, that's not what I'm tawlkin' about. You know

that the seminar folk and the ELITE wish that we would go away. We all know that. I just get this feelin' that somethin' is up."

"Well, I have you to know, Jesus," came the supported voice of one hillbilly. *"Sticks and stones may break my bones, but their words don't mean nothin'! You can count on me."*

"Me, too!" Came a second.
"Me, three!" And then a third.
"Me, four!" A fourth and so-on.

Everyone was eager to stand there beside Jesus.

This was a proud lot.

Shorty then chimed in, *"Jesus, ever since the first day you told me and EveylynAnn about God's goot news, I have believed ya with my heart and all of my gizzard. Though the road has been rocky at times, you've taken us to the top. Count me in, too!"*

"Thanks, Shorty," Jesus said, *"but be careful. Things are always easier in a room of similar minds. The trick is to be faithful when they ain't. You'll know what I mean when you are cooped up with a bunch of wolves and they are lookin' at ya like ya are a Rhode Island Red!"*

They ate and ate.

During the meal, each remembered when they first heard and experienced God's goot news. To top off the meal, Jesus passed the RC Colas and Moonpies.

Then they sang.

"Amazing Grace."
"Beulah Land."
"When I Saw the Light."

And even a chorus of *"Rocky Top"* was rumored to be one of the tunes sung that night.

They then strolled toward the Bicentennial Park.

(14:27-42)
Hit's Hard to Pray with a Full Belly

There Jesus again repeated that somethin' was up.

He axed 'em to pray for peace.
He implored 'em to pray for all hillbillies.
And they all prayed because somethin' was up.
The gravy was being stirred.
Each was afraid of what might happen.
Each had followed Jesus out of a heart's desire to be a part of God's freedom for demselves and the world. They committed demselves to God's savin' grace that would restore God's love within 'em and others through a grace that is preventin', convictin', justifyin', and sanctifyin'--and in this life time. They noed John Wesley's sermon of *"The Scripture Way of Salvation"* almost by heart. They had opened themselves to the notion that God ain't satisfied with just redeemin'! God's in the restorin' business as well.

Whereas the Hillbilly Augustine understood

people's taintedness humanity as an act of sassing God, these hillbillies had been convinced people had forgotten to love 'demselves and God alike.[151] They swam, now, in the clear waters of God's grace. Those waters was Gilead's balm. They lived as though God was plantin' new thangs within that would change 'em into lovin' hillbillies. They took deep pride in livin' in the notion that love is the final goal of their salvation. They just didn't want to believe, they wanted to love.[152] Jesus held school with 'em, learnin' em that this love had to be a practice, a practice with others. This they knew, but tonight it didn't seem that clear. Jesus, too, prayed, *"God, somethin' is up and I'm not sure what. I hope that no one gets hurt. Even me. But whatever happens, I'm yours."*

After more prayin' and studyin,' Jesus looked around and found everyone asleep.

Once your belly is full and your body gets warm, sleep will get a holt of ya and overtake all of your being right down to your gizzard!

Jesus prayed again.

The hillbillies continued to sleep.

It must have been durin' this second time of prayin' and studyin' that Pat slipped out, unnoticed, to add a little flour to the gravy.

---

[151] See Melvin E. Dieter, et al. *Five Views on Sanctification* (Grand Rapids, MI: Zondervan Publishing House, 1987), 22-3.

[152] See Deiter, 27.

(14:43-52)
Hit's Time to Test the Gravy

As Jesus finished prayin', the SAM Army surrounded the sleepin' hillbillies. There along with 'em were the members of the ELITE and their cronies.

In between them stood Pat.

Pat had worked out a plan that would now require Jesus to respond.

"It's time to test the gravy," Pat said confidently to hisself, SAM, and God.

Now remember that Pat had only plotted this in order for the whole town to know what Jesus was talkin' about in terms of what God was about to do. This incident would raise Jesus to a higher profile, or so was Pat's plan. God's goot news would no longer be confined to a bunch of hillbillies, but would become part of the whole world. Mainstream was his goal.

Pat went up to Jesus and shook his hand, whisperin' in his ear, *"It's time! I know ya can do it!"*

With that signal, Jesus was arrested.

By now, the sleepin' hillbillies had been disturbed from their slumber. The rattlin' of handcuffs will do that. However, no one moved for they were frozen by the fear that paralyzed.

"I see ya'll come for an outlaw!" Jesus said to the officers as he was handcuffed.

No one said a word.

Pat was waitin' for Jesus to make his move.

Jesus was taken across the street to the county jail.

A young boy, whose father was born and raised in Townsend, followed Jesus to the jail-house. The boy was interested in what was a happenin'.

The hillbillies remained back at the park.

The officials grabbed the boy by the shirt, but fear of arrest and distrust of authorities overcame him. His shirt was ripped as he ran away! Today, most people think that boy now lives in West Hills.

Jesus was booked and jailed for unlawful assembly.

Pat was still waitin'!

(14:52-72)
Guilty as Sin

The next day Jesus was arraigned on charges of *"unlawful assembly, inciting a riot, and a being a public nuisance."*

Someone in the crowd shouted to the judge, *"Throw the book at him, Judge. He ain't done nothin' but stir up a hornet's nest. Besides, all those hoodlums hangin' around him and around here can't be good."*

"Jesus?" the judged axed. *"Do you understand the charges? Do you want to enter a plea?"*

"I reckon so," Jesus replied, *"I guess if'n it's wrong to sleep at Bicentennial Park, and if'n it's wrong for a bunch*

of folk to travel around together, and if'n it's wrong for people to have hope and faith in the possibility of new starts and new lives made possible by God's freedom, then I'm guilty. I'm guilty as sin. Throw the book at me!"

By now Shorty had shed his red-plaid flannel and swapped it for a button-down, light-blue Oxford shirt. He quietly pushed his way into the crowded courtroom. A person nearby asked if he was one of those hillbillies. *"Do I look like one? Surely ya can tell by the way I dress that I'm not part of 'em,"* he replied.

Suddenly, he remembered Jesus's words.

He felt that he was different from everyone else.

He felt like a chicken in a den of wolves.

Shorty quickly left the court room and ran into the bathroom. Splashin' cold water into his face hopin' to awake from what felt like a nightmare, he looked into the mere above the wash-basin.

Lookin' made him sick to his stomach.

He was sick 'cause he was betrayin' his hillbilly heritage.

He ran to the toilet and threw-up.
Afterwards, he cried like he had never cried before. The flow of tears at first shocked him, but what shocked him was that he wanted to cry even more.

(15:1-47)
Crucified in the Papers
    The next day the media had a field day with both the arrest and subsequent guilty admission. One columnist devoted his print space to write that religion in the South is guided solely on emotion and ignorance. *"Anybody will follow anybody in the name of God,"* the columnist began. *"If you tied a bale of hay to a Ford Pick-up and drove it down Main Street, half of Knoxvul would be following and claim that the Messiah had done come. Let's be reasonable, people."*
    The editor addressed the fact that Jesus had done no real harm. What Jesus lacked, the editor added, was an understandin' about the facts of economics and the ability of the free market that could assist the hillbilly. If Jesus would stop criticizin' the way things are and put his faith in Adam Smith. *"What Jesus needs to remember is that God has given us a true and authentic model for business,"* the article stated. *"Faith must be rooted in the invisible and benevolent hand of mechanical economics.*[153] *Free trade is the way that this invisible hand works. It can coordinate socioeconomic life in such a way that the common good would best be served by an economic morality of principled self-interest."*
    This writer was well acquainted with his god.
    "The quicker that Jesus and others learn this valuable

---

[153] See Adam Smith, *An Inquiry Into the Nature and Causes of the Wealth of Nations* (originally published in 1776) *Great Books of the Western World* (Chicago: Encyclopedia Britannica, Inc. 1990), 194.

lesson, the sooner that hard work and the American dream will truly pay its dividends," the editor said in conclusion.

No need to physically hurt Jesus.

Indifference and trivializin' proves to be more powerful and most effective.

A letter in reply to the editor simply suggested that what was wrong with Jesus was his communist ideas and leanin's. *"His ladder always did learn against the wrong wall,"* the reply concluded.

Editorial cartoons depicted him a king sitting upon the wooden seat of an outhouse. With a Sears and Roebuck as his scepter in his right hand and a corncob in the other, Jesus was called the *"Potentate of the Pitiful Hillbilly."*

Radio talk shows were filled with both pro and con remarks about the teachin's of this Jesus. One lone voice posed a question for reflection: *"If a person feeds the hungry, befriends the friendless, and clothes the naked, everybody calls that person a saint. However, if a person asks why people are hungry, why people are friendless and why people are naked, then why is that person is called a rebel?"*

To that came no response.

Pat was still waiting for both Jesus and God to make their moves.

Jesus must have felt quite alone that night. He as much as said it to be so!

He was a man who only wanted people to

experience God's freein' power.

Yet, for the most part, he was portrayed as either a rebel or lunatic with delusory tendencies. During the night, Jesus died. It was at midnight. Pitch dark. No one knew why he died, but some knew how. Jesus was found "strung-up" with a make shift noose made out of orange jail pants. The door to his cell had been found ajar.

Rumors spread like wild fire. You've heard the stories, the rumors, and tales. Each seemed both valid and absurd at the same time. Though never verified, it was said that at precisely midnight, the lone dogwood tree in the county courtyard was filled with white blossoms. Maybe that was just another rumor.

Jesus was to be given a pauper's burial, reported the local paper.

A member of the Church of High Society said that he wanted to give more dignity to Jesus and the whole situation. He offered to pick up the tab, as well as make the arrangements. The town quickly took up the offer. (Spendin' money on a pauper is a financial liability that can raise taxes, you noed.) The church member took the body to McCarty's Mortuary for preparation of burial.

Mary from Maryville, along with another Mary from Michigan, found out where he had been taken.

"HE AIN'T HERE!"

(16:1-8)

He Ain't Here! And Things Are Goin' to be Different!

Now, the two Marys went the next day to the mortuary to pay their respects. They brought a vial of homemade rose perfume with 'em.

It was real early.

It was so early that no one was at the funeral home.

At first, they thought that they would have to go back home but they found a door ajar and walked in. The place smelled of old flowers and seemed heavy with unanswered prayers. They searched each parlor until they found the one that was marked "Jesus."

At the rear of the room was the coffin.

They approached it deliberately and cautiously.

They gently pried open the coffin lid, but they quickly and disappointedly discovered that it was empty.

"What has happened? Where is our Jesus?" they exclaimed.

"Don't be afraid!" a voice came boomin' from behind them.

They had no idea that anyone else was around. They were startled to the point of wettin' their pants, but retained 'demselves.

They turned 180 degrees.

"If you're lookin' for Jesus, he ain't here. God has

done gone made God's move! Jesus ain't here!" proclaimed the young boy with a torn white shirt.

"Looks like a hillbilly," thought Mary from Michigan to herself.

"He ain't here," he repeated, *"He was. But he ain't now. Go and tell the rest of the hillbillies that things are really different now!"*

So they left, runnin'!

And without speaking a word.

Stunned silence was the rule and they were amazed at their silence.

They didn't say a word. They just ran.

(16:9-19)

Postscript

They later told all the hillbillies what happened at the funeral home. Immediately after that, the message of God's goot news of a lynched but raised, Jesus was proclaimed by and amongst God's hillbillies.

Now God defeated the powers of death on the first day of the week. This was first made known to Mary from Maryville and Mary from Michigan, who experienced first-hand God's move of raisin' Jesus from the dead.

They went out tellin' more people about God's freein' notion.

It was hard for some to use their 20/20 ears at first.

Fear is a powerful power to overcome.

More people through 'em knew God's freedom.
In the country sides.
In the cities.
Still some don't believe. They haven't believed 'cause they haven't yet had the experience of the risen Jesus and God's freein' notion!

To this day in the midst of the rollin' hollers and in the peaks and ridges of the Smoky Mountains you can still hear the echoes of Jesus' words, *"Go into all the hills, hollers, alleys, towns, cities, and suburbs and tell of the new creation that is possible by God's goot news! To those who believe and follow, they shall be my hillbillies!*

And they shall be free and powerful! Free to be! Powerful with love!

In God's name, they shall be able to cast out the demonic spirit of oppression and hate. They shall speak commandin' words of hope and promise; they shall have the courage to take holt of the most deadly of people and have power over poisonous words of hate and bigotry, and they shall live and be transformed! They shall be able to lay hands on those who lack love and who need a strong accepting embrace, and they shall be made whole!"

To this day, the hillbilly, God's hillbilly is the established and confirmed sign of God's love and that God is redeemin' and transformin' this world.

God has gone and done somethin' special with the people of the mountains, the hillbillies.

Today there are many folks who claimed the mountains as home. God, however, done gone and loved these mountains and its people long ago when no one else would have either of 'em.

WORDS AFTER HAND

Go into all the hills, hollers, alleys, towns, cities, and suburbs and tell of the new creation that is possible by God's goot news! To those who believe and follow, they shall be my hillbillies!

And they shall be free and powerful! Free to be! Powerful with love!

In God's name, they shall be able to cast out the demonic spirit of oppression and hate. They shall speak commandin' words of hope and promise; they shall have the courage to take holt of the most deadly of people and have power over poisonous words of hate and bigotry, and they shall live and be transformed! They shall be able to lay lands on those who lack love and who need a strong accepting embrace, and they shall be made whole!

The Gospel According to John Bill Bob Mark, Smoky Mountain Version (SMV)

"I love to testify," I said into the microphone, "but I've never preached before. I just want you to know that I submit myself to your authority, Brother Carl. You're the pastor of this church, and if I step out of the Word, I want you to tell me." He smiled back and nodded. He would.

The choice of text was simple--the chapter the handlers believed so deeply, they were risking their lives to confirm it. "Let's look at Mark 16," I said.

"Amen," Carl replied. He was pulling for me....

"It was after they crucified Jesus," I said, "and some of the women who had stayed with him through it all came down to the tomb to anoint his body with spices. Am I in the Word?" I looked over to Brother Carl.

"You're in the Word," Carl said.[154]

Salvation on Sand Mountain: Snake Handling and Redemption in Southern Appalachia,
Dennis Covington

---

[154] Dennis Covington, *Salvation on Sand Mountain: Snake Handling and Redemption in Southern Appalachia.* (New York: Addison-Wesley Publishing Company, 1992), 23.

The year was 1991.
The place was Scottsboro, Alabama.
The arrival of autumn in the South means the changing of the colors of the eye-catching foliage and breathe-taking revivals of the fall. The advent of crisp cool mornings, that replace the hot and humid beginnings of southern summers, announces that there is something different in the air.
Glendel Buford Summerford, a minister of the gospel and local snake handler preacher on Sand Mountain in northeastern Alabama, had been found guilty of attempted murder. A jury had been convinced that Summerford tried to kill his wife, Darlene, by forcing her to place an arm in a box of rattlesnakes. At gunpoint, he compelled her to expose her unprotected forearms in the cramped box of the deadly creatures. She was bitten twice and nearly died.
Summerford was found guilty and sentenced to ninety-nine years of prison.
Dennis Covington, *New York Times* journalist, was one of many journalists who covered the trial. In covering the story, he found, at least for himself, much more than just the facts about a trial of a snake-handling preacher and the jury's verdict.
Facts are meaningful only in the context of a story.
Covington enters an exploration of self-discovery amidst the mountain life of southern

Appalachia where choreographed acts of snake handling and consumption of poisonous drink seem both foreign and all too familiar. In his book, *Salvation on Sand Mountain*, Covington reveals the nuances and subtleties of religious expressions that are somewhat unique and peculiar to rural southern Appalachia.

By no means the norm nor representative of all mountain people, Covington records the world of a faith community that embraces life in full - handling rattlesnakes, casting out of demons, speaking in tongues, drinking strychnine, and subjecting their flesh to the penetrating heat of a hand-held blow torch. Such life-threatening acts, which appear to be inflictions of personal brutality and harm, are but communal gestures of social solidarity against an enemy - a foe - an evil that is experienced as larger than life and twice as powerful. The worship, however, is also a celebration of an even more powerful God who can bind the powers of that evil foe of enmity. Though bizarre and grotesque on the surface, this Christian expression of faith is more about both the nature of God and the nature of God's people than snake boxes, Mason jars, exorcisms, and glossolalia.

Caught in the cultural collision of a past history of self-sufficiency, reinforced through the experience of nurtured individualism on one hand, while on the other, effects of economic and social exploitation, these mountaineers experience the world in the context of "bad news"--rootlessness, angst, and powerlessness. Bad news far too often is identified as "Uncle Sam." For this people who handle snakes, drink poison, and voluntarily burn themselves with torches however, God's "good news" is found in Mark 16. It is not only good, but it also has real effects!

The world and worship that includes snake handling was quite different than Covington's traditional quiet and guarded Methodist upbringing in an urban residential neighborhood of Birmingham. Apart from an occasional enthusiastic preacher, religious life was far tamer and safer than that on Sand Mountain. However, after baptizing himself in the world that was once so strange, he discovers his own mountain roots. He discovers that he is only two generations removed from the mountains, from the same mountain and the same people!

> You see, growing up in [urban residential Birmingham], where people were trying so hard to escape their humble pasts, I had come of age not knowing much about my family history....I would discover that Covingtons had not always lived in Birmingham, but that at some point we, too, had come down from the mountains, and that those wild-eyed, perspiring preachers of my childhood were kin to me in a way I could never have expected nor fully appreciated. In retrospect, I believe that my religious education had pointed me all along toward some ultimate

rendezvous with people who took up serpents.[155]

Covington finds himself so much "back home," nevertheless, that he begins to immerse himself in the event and experience of worship as opposed to being just a spectator and observer. He handles a snake, once, and is caught in its mesmerizing hypnotic salve of power and control. Handling a creature that has the power to take life is both frightening and exciting. *"I had actually envisioned myself preaching out of my car with a Bible, a trunk load of rattlesnakes, and a megaphone...."* [156]

Amidst the changing foliage, snake handling meetings, and revivals, Covington found himself caught in between the worlds of his upbringing and this mountain people. Something different was in the air.

Covington concludes his book by telling of the experience of an invitation to preach at an evening service.

It was an invitation that was earned.
It would be Covington's first sermon.
It would be his last.

Along with the invitation, however, is the assumption that he will remain faithful to the "tradition" and to the "Word." He knows that Brother Carl, the church's pastor who has extended

---

[155] Ibid., 10-11.
[156] Ibid., 236.

this privilege, will be both judge and jury.

"But the stone had been rolled away from the tomb," I said, "and a man in white, an angel, was sitting there, and the angel said to the women: 'He's not here. He's risen.' Am I in the Word?"

"Amen," Carl said. "You're in the Word."

"I'm in the Word," I repeated, and I moved along the platform like I'd seen Carl do so many times. "And who did Jesus appear to first after his resurrection?"

"The eleven," Carl said.

I turn back to him. "No. He didn't appear first to the eleven." And I walked slowly across the platform again, heading straight for Carl's son Virgil, who was standing by his drum set, sticks crossed in front of him. "He appeared first to Mary Magdalene!" I said, and I drove each word in the direction of Virgil's chest with my finger. "A woman out of whom he had cast seven devils."

There was no amen.

I whirled back around and faced the congregation again.

"The angel had told her to tell the disciples that Jesus was risen, but she was afraid, and she didn't do it. So Jesus himself appeared to her, and when she told the disciples that he had risen, none of the men believed her!"

I was waiting for an amen, which still hadn't come.

"That's when Jesus appeared to the eleven and upbraided them for their unbelief!"

"Amen," Carolyn Porter, Carl's wife, finally said.

I knew I was in the Word now. It was close to the feeling I'd had when I'd handled.[157]

Is the Smoky Mountain Version of the Gospel of Mark in the "Word?"
Is it faithful to the "tradition?"

---

[157] Ibid., 231-2.

One early reader of this SMV returned the manuscript to me almost as quickly as I had hand delivered it. She said that she could not and would not read it after a short but quick survey of the first page.

"Why?" I inquired inquisitively and guardedly.

"Well, if you must know," she responded. *"I believe that God's word is so true that to attempt to alter it in any way is disrespectful. I will not read something that disrespects the 'Word of God.' And I can't read it because knowing that it is wrong I would only be inviting a judgment upon me."*

The SMV does not "respect" word for word the Gospel of Mark, admittedly. It is a paraphrase at best and an embellishment at worst, I confess.

But is it in the "Word?"

Does it disrespect God's truth?

Life is a "tensed existence," with a past, present, and future.

Though "facts" are used to describe the past, present, and future, it takes a story to give it form and significance. Life, therefore, is at least narrative in form. Narrative is the form or means in which that life is told, presented, and by which meaning is assessed.

The basic structure of God's story is narrative as well.

God's story includes a "faith-ing" community with a history, culture, and identity. In the case of the Christian community, God's story is about a man called Jesus of Nazareth who lived, was killed, and then resurrected by God. This Jesus is not simply a "point" to be made by God. Jesus is the point, so to speak. As in all communities, a commonly held story forges, molds, and knits together its members. The Christian community is not just a collection of individuals and unrelated people, but is a culture defined, nurtured, and swayed by that story of God who is manifested in the wooden cross of a first-century Palestine Jew by the name of Jesus.

Narrative provides meaning and a sense of belonging, because it is confessional in nature. According to H. Richard Niebuhr, the *"preaching of the early Christian church was not an argument for the existence of God nor an admonition to follow the dictates of some common human conscience, unhistorical and super-social in character. It was primarily a simple recital of the great events connected with the historical appearance of Jesus Christ and a confession of what had happened to the community of disciples."* [158]

In other words, Christian scriptures contain the story of a community that not only experiences the risen Jesus, but also attempts to articulate the

---

[158] H. Richard Niebuhr. "The Story of Our Life," Stanley Hauerwas and L. Gregory Jones, eds. *Why Narrative? Readings in Theology* (Grand Rapids, MI: W. B. Eerdmans, 1989), 21.

meaning of that experience. The early Christian gospel stories more than tell this story; they confess a faith and a commitment to it. Though God's story contains factual and objective facts or events, its purpose is more than bookish chronicling. It is a story with a theological foundation of meaning, a sense of belonging, and mission. The Christian story has purpose before it has a purpose. It doesn't make a point of meaning, belonging, and mission. Its point is meaning, belonging, and mission. That's my hope for the SMV.

Hence, according to Hans Frei, *"faith is not based on factual evidence or inherent historical likelihood."* [159] Rather, faith emerges out of the intersection of the personal and communal life story of an individual and God's story as revealed in the life, death, and resurrection of Jesus of Nazareth. The text of God's story presents the reader and hearer with a clash of two worlds. One is the subjective world of the reader-hearer and the other is the world of the gospel story. In the SMV, the world of Appalachia of Junior and EvelynAnn clashes with the world of God's "freein' notion."

Since the biblical narrative is a story in the language of the "folk," that claims that God's story is accessible, experiential, and palatable. Faith is the connection between the "inner history" of the

---

[159] Hans W. Frei. *The Identity of Jesus Christ* (Eugene, OR: Wipf and Stock Publishers, 1997), 183.

subjective world of the reader-hearer and the "outer history" of the chronicle of God's revelation. Narrative theology is a way and means of talking about that intersection. Therefore reader is automatically included in the story, argues Michael Root. Since the reader-hearer does not exist in isolation, there is a "storied relation" within the Christian narrative.[160] Mott notes that *"...[t]he stories of Jesus and of the reader are related by the narrative connections that make them two sequences within a single larger story.* **These storied relations, rather than general truths the story illustrates, mediate between the story and reader. The story is good news because redemption follows from the primary form of inclusion in the story** (emphasis added)."[161]

For the SMV, the hillbilly is included as well. God's story of Jesus is "what it means," to borrow a phrase from Tex Sample. It does have a point; the story is one of freedom, meaning, redemption, and belonging. In the context of the SMV, God's story provides meaning of and to the expressions of welcome, extensions of hospitality, assertions of acceptance, and a call to become one of God's hillbillies by immersing oneself in God's freedom to be, simply be.

---

[160] Michael Root, "The Narrative Structure of Soteriology," Stanley Hauerwas and L. Gregory Jones, eds. *Why Narrative? Readings in Theology* (Grand Rapids, MI: W. B. Eerdmans, 1989), 266.

[161] Ibid.

The efficacy of such hospitality, freedom, and calling is that believers are *"grateful and obedient sons and daughters...called to be in the breadth of our private and public lives, in our prayers, in the church, and in the world. The name and identity of Jesus Christ, set forth in the narrative of the New Testament, call upon the believer for nothing less than this discipleship,"* [162]

The Jesus of the Smoky Mountain Version of Mark can ask nothing less either.

The SMV is based on an approach to biblical interpretation that is "relational" in its assumption and "interactive" in its method.

This approach is based upon the work of Fredrick C. Tiffany and Sharon H. Ringe[163] and the assumption that "truth" of scripture emerges from the intersection of reader and text. Therefore "truth" is not a kernel that is extracted from the shell of superfluous sheathing which its only purpose is to "protect" and "guard" the integrity of its core. Such "shelling" presupposes that the casing is dispensable and of no merit apart from its intrinsic value of insulation. The method posed by Tiffany and Ringe suggests that "truth" emerges out of "relating." *"Meaning thus occurs not in isolated words or signs, but in the relationships of those words within and between the worlds...."* [164]

---

[162] Frei, 194-5.

[163] Frederick C. Tiffany and Sharon H. Ringe. *Biblical Interpretation: A Roadmap* (Nashville: Abingdon Press, 1996).

[164] Ibid., 27.

So as I explored Mark's gospel, "truth" was not limited to simple or complex biblical analysis.

"Truth" emerged from both Mark's world and my world. However, it is important to note the "grammar" of the biblical tradition. Walter Brueggemann suggests that the biblical text is *"so powerful and compelling, so passionate and uncompromising in its anguish and hope that it requires we submit our experience to it and thereby reenter our experience on new terms, namely the terms of the text."* [165] The faith tradition of the biblical record, therefore, requires that I "submit" my experience to the interpretation as yielded by the text, not vise versa. This is the "grammar" of the SMV with the text of Mark as the subject and my southern Appalachia roots the object.

It is not enough just to "know" the world of Jesus, nor simply my own world. Biblical interpretation mapping requires interchange, *"Since meaning occurs in the interaction between the text and those who receive it, and is not defined or delimited by the text alone, each new occasion with a text will create new meanings."* [166] This perspective even holds for the same person and same community in different times.

It seems rather strange but true, though. I never seriously inquired nor engaged my family's

---

[165] Walter Brueggemann, *A Commentary on Jeremiah: Exile and Homecoming.* (Grand Rapids, Michigan: William B. Eerdmans Publishing Company, 1998), 18.

[166] Tiffany and Ringe, 27.

story, or even my own, until I began hearing the "gospel story."

It was in a high school class assignment that I began to unearth some of my familial roots in folks like Jacob, Daniel, Juliana, William Oliver, Carrie, Stanley Freeman, and Willard John, who would later change his name to John Willard. My discovery was more than just "facts" though. What began to emerge for my benefit was a story of stories about some German and Irish immigrants forging an unknown future, beginning with wanderings from a seaport in Philadelphia, Pennsylvania, to following the riches and demands of in-laws to Knoxville, Tennessee, where whiskey and church were among the most important aspects of community life.

It was in the hearing of the gospel story and experience of love, grace, and freedom at a small United Methodist congregation that my life story also unearthed some far more numerous "familial" roots in folks like Abraham, Sarah, Hagar, Ishmael, Issac, Rebekah, Jacob, Essau, Leah, Rachel, Martha, Peter, Mary, and Jesus, along with a multitude others. Meaning and a sense of belonging began to dawn. My own personhood was both respected and nurtured.

The intersection between the story of people and the story of God is best articulated and conveyed through narration, not just facts. My family is much more than a collection of facts. The facts of my family life are held together by a story of stories.

I am a southerner and have descended from the area of southern Appalachia, hillbilly land.
This is the land of summer afternoons spent sipping iced-tea.
Land of supper tables graced with greens.
It is home of the Bible belt which has no jean-loops in which to thread.
Also, it includes the confederate flag.
It is the land of my southern birth. I am a southerner by birth and choice.

When I discovered I had a choice, I didn't think being a southerner was all that I had been lead to believe! I did not like the "fact" of my hillbilly heritage.

When I went to college, I did everything humanly possible to "disavow" my heritage as a "redneck hillbilly." As a second generation removed from the Appalachia Mountains, I grew up in the middle of classical country music, white socks, tee shirts, and jeans. Though not a racecar fan, I had an uncle who used to race on a dirt track outside of Knoxville. My dad was a "grease-monkey." He could fix anything from a lawnmower to a propeller engine plane.

My southern upbringing reminded me, however, that I belonged to a family. Though uprooted because my father was a "lifer" in the Air Force, our "family values" were such that no matter what, I could always count on the love of my parents and siblings. Nothing, absolutely nothing, could ever dismantle, tear, or break that bond. It was as strong as steel from Birmingham, unlike the "pot-metal" from up North. One Appalachian value, however, handed down to me was the distrust of others. Whereas it served as an instrument to insure survival in the mountains, when dislodged from the hills, it becomes a source of suspicion, uneasiness, and cultural bias. It has the effect of making it difficult to love others, even one's self.

College was a new and eye-opening experience.

I was introduced to classical music.

Instead of Hank Williams, it was Bach.

Instead of Cline, Wynettee, and Homer and Jethro, it was Chopin, Beethoven, and Pachelbel.

Philosophical thought was a "new way" for me to think and reflect about life. Instead of Grandma Moses and Uncle Jimmy, I read Plato, Socrates, Hume, Bacon, Kierkegaard, and Kant.

Within economics, the new worlds of Karl Marx and John Adams were personalities, ideas, and worlds that, though they sat at opposite spectrums that often collided, both shared some common interests about wealth distribution.

Part of my education made me keenly aware

that "southerners," though hospitable and polite, are sometimes considered part of the "backwaters" of American life.

I wanted to fit into my new world.

So off came the white socks.

My radio found a new station dial.

I started a personal library and even read most of the books that were often windows into worlds that seemed so far from my own. The further the world, the better the read.

Life experiences, however, have pushed me to be more accepting of who I am and where I come from. It has been, however, my experience of the risen Christ and his community, that has taught me about familial loyalty, heritage, and to whom I belong. The insights and theology of John Wesley has instructed me about God's freedom. It led me to be convinced that I am loved and can be transformed into a loving being by the God who redeems, frees, and changes.

There is no hotter topic south of the Mason-Dixon line than the subject surrounding the public demonstration and use of the Confederate flag. The struggle with the symbol evokes passions of both loyalty and hatred, and it does so with plenty of company.

The Confederate flag is about loyalty and heritage.

It is about a loyalty to a people, a terrain and

region, and a culture "representative" of the South in some "pristine" notion.

I also need to be frank and honest, it is also about hatred, bigotry, and violence.

The Pre-Civil War South was the arena for legitimized slave labor. It is also the land of "Jim Crow" laws in Post-Civil War times. We have a lot to learn about race relations. The argument that the Civil War was really about "states' rights," not slavery, is misleading. "States' rights" only makes sense if the issue was about a state's right to have slavery. Either way, it fails the "gospel" principle of love, community, and issues of freedom. The gospel does not define the limits of God's love based upon skin color, social/economic status, gender, nor sexual orientation. The gospel is the proclamation that God freely loves and transforms. God redeems and forgives. The experience enables the overcoming of shame in order that a declaration of freedom can be made. "Race" seems to set the tone, pace, and character of the South. Of course, it can be said of the North, or any part of the United States of America, as well. All too often, life in the South gets divided along those lines.

The first time I read James Cone's *God of the Oppressed*,[167] I said, "Amen!" My "amen" came out of both my educated bias of "liberal guilt," but also

---

[167] James Cone. *God of the Oppressed* (New York: Orbis Press, 1997).

and more importantly, out of a sense that Cone was speaking my language, the same language of oppressed white folk, i.e., "hillbillies," at least to a degree. It was like discovering that here is family that has always lived next door and I didn't know it. As Jim Goad suggests, *"For economic reasons, the trash--be it black, brown, or white--have always lived side by side in America. It's the Gold Card Whites who've always paid to segregate themselves, leaving the rednecks, niggers, and spics to fight over day-old cookies"* [168]

At this point, I need to offer a caveat.

While I quote Goad directly, I need to make sure that his use of "redneck, nigger, and spic" is rightly understood. I see his use of such "vulgar" epitaphs for the purpose of "cultural location" not "racial slurring." I value his directness in that he is addressing the issue of class-ism that gets lost in contemporary discussions about "race." Through the lens of liberation theology, I conclude that Goad is speaking with "God's preferential option for the poor," i.e., the lower class. Though Goad is a skeptic of religion and its institutional incarnations, he seems to be speaking of the same "trashing" phenomenal that Cone's God has the power to redeem and free.

The Gospel of Mark, for me and the community of faith I call home, speaks of a God who not only redeems "trash" but who can use

---

[168] Jim Goad. *The Redneck Manifesto* (New York: Touchstone, 1997), 35.

"trash" to redeem the rest of the world. That's "goot" news for a hillbilly like myself who is *"pissed because there are some who are so well-off while there are so many who have it so bad!"*

This is what Jesus is about.

This is what the SMV is about. It takes "seriously" and "playfully" the *parable* that "reversal is the essence of redemption."[169]

This parable is powerful because in the South, it has always been known that the white aristocracy of imperialism has used its power to *"divide and conquer...For most of America's history, [white imperialism] worked at getting rednecks to blame the niggers. For the past thirty years or so, they've encouraged the niggers to blame the rednecks. This is for certain: If the niggers and rednecks ever joined forces, they'd be unbeatable."* [170]

The character of a hillbilly Jesus carries the heavy baggage of extreme hope. Is it possible, as Newitz and Wray suggest, that white trash just might be *"one place multiculturalism might look for a white identity which does not view itself as the norm from which all other races and ethnicities divide?"* [171] Is such a perspective possible? Is such a hope a probability? A hillbilly Jesus raises the possibility, at least. The possibility is that "white trash" can be a "corrective" to the

---

[169] See Kathleen A. Robertson Farmer. "The Book of Ruth," *The New Interpreter's Bible, Volume II* (Nashville: Abingdon Press, 1998), 892.

[170] Ibid., 32.

[171] Matt Wray and Annalee Newitz, eds. *White Trash: Race and Class in America*. (New York: Routledge, 1997), 5.

assumption that *"whiteness must always equal terror and racism."* [172]

In short, it is because of my southern upbringing and not in spite of it, that I say it is time to acknowledge the pain and horror of slavery and denounce the symbol that was used to legitimate a philosophical theory palatable for "Christian consumption." I do not need the Confederate flag because as a Christian, I claim a higher loyalty because it has claimed me.

Come to think of it, the flag of the United States, as well, is all too prominent and visible in our churches. We have come to believe that our loyalties to God are somewhat "conditioned" and "tempered" by nationalism.

To whom do our loyalties belong?

And to whom do we belong?

Is it time to raise the banner of God's redeeming and transforming love above any other?

These are just a few of the questions confronting the writing and composition of the SMV.

As I have discovered, it has the power to take this "redneck hillbilly", to convince him that he is not only loved, but God can change him into a "loving redneck hillbilly." Now that's Wesleyan!

I am thankful and grateful for the new life that has come to me in Jesus and his community.

---

[172] Ibid.

Imagine that!

The SMV is about my family.
It is about my people.
It is about me.
It is also about those totally different from me.

It is about God's story in Jesus intersecting the life of a resurrected "red-neck hillbilly" who has heard his named called to become one of God's hillbillies.

Covington was within reach of his preaching limits and also on the verge of discovering God's truth as it re-entered his life. This is how he finished that first, if not last sermon.

> I knew I was in the Word now. It was close to the feeling I'd had when I'd handled. "Mary Magdalene was the first person to spread the news of the risen Christ!" I shouted. "She was the first evangelist, and the men didn't even believe her! So when we start talking about a woman's place, we better add that a woman's place is to preach the gospel of Jesus Christ! In Him there is no male or female, no Greek or Jew!" And I spun on Carl. "Am I in the Word?"
> "No," Carl said. "You're not in the Word."
> "Are you telling me I'm out of the Word?"
> "Yes, You're out of the Word." He smiled. It was a smile of enormous satisfaction and relief....
> "Well, if I'm out of the Word," I said, "I'd better stop preaching."[173]

---

[173] Covington, 232.

As Covington would later conclude, his preaching experience was not about the role of women as it was about the nature of God. It is about the nature of God who welcomes, who calls, who loves, and who frees. The experience took Covington back to his childhood experience in East Lake and to his childhood neighborhood, where he had grown up not knowing the identity of his ancestry.

> It's late afternoon at the lake. The turtles are moving closer to shore. The surface of the water is undisturbed, an expanse of smooth, gray slate. Their mothers call most of the children in my neighborhood home for supper. They open the back doors, wipe their hands on their aprons and yell, "Willie!" or "Joe!" or "Ray!" Either that or they use a bell, bolted to the doorframe and loud enough to start the dogs barking in backyards all along the street. But I was always called home by my father, and he didn't do it in the customary way. He walked down the alley all the way to the lake. If I was close, I could hear his shoes on the gravel before he came into sight. If I was far, I would see him across the surface of the water, emerging out of shadows and into the gray light. He would stand with his hands in the pockets of his windbreaker while he looked for me. This is how he got me to come home. He always came to the place where I was before he called my name.[174]

The SMV is about such a calling and such freedom.

It is about God coming to the our places and calling us by name.

---

[174] Ibid., 239-40.

God comes and calls us by name.

When all is said and done, God simply came to the place where I was before and called me by my hillbilly name.

Am I in the "Word?"

"The Word of God for the people of God!"
"Thanks be to God!"

ISBN 1553958883-7

9 781553 958833